From Award-winning, best-selling author
Denise Domning

SEASON OF THE FOX

PRAISE FOR THE FIRST
SERVANT OF THE CROWN MYSTERY,
SEASON OF THE RAVEN

"In this medieval mystery of stunning realism, Domning brings the English countryside alive with all the rich detail of a Bosch painting. With well realized characters and a depth of historical detail, she creates a vibrant mystery and

*Friend of
the Library Donor*

Donated by
Lana Wong
SCC Librarian

RAISE THE HUE AND CRY!

A wealthy merchant has been murdered in his own home, and the suspect has fled to sanctuary in a local church. Enter Sir Faucon de Ramis, the king's new Servant of the Crown in the shire, to solve the murder, assisted by his prickly secretary, Brother Edmund.

As Faucon begins his hunt, the shire's the new Crowner finds himself in the upside down world of a woman's trade. Not only does the merchant's wife own the business–Unheard of! –the suspect is the daughter's betrothed, or so the town believes. But what about the bloody shoe prints and missing tally sticks at the scene, and what does the sheriff have to gain?

Other books

Season of the Fox

DENISE
DOMNING

SEASON OF THE FOX

Copyright © Denise Domning 2015

ISBN-13: 978-1508676614
ISBN-10: 1508676615

EDITED BY: Martha Stites

ORIGINAL COVER ART:
Ms Sloane 2435, f.85 'Cleric, Knight and Workman representing the three classes, illustration from 'Li Livres dou Sante' (vellum), French School, (13th century)/ British Library, London, UK/©British Library Board. All Rights Reserved/The Bridgeman Art Library

DESIGN: Denise Domning

Printed in the United States of America, First paperback edition: March, 2015

My Apologies

My apologies to the people of Warwickshire. I have absconded with your county, added cities that don't exist and parsed your history to make it suit my needs. Outside of that, I've done my best to keep my recreation of England in the 12th Century as accurate as possible.

Dedication

To my dear friend Gail Haugland.
Thank you for being there for me over
this difficult year and for letting me use
your husband as a model for one of the
characters in this book.

horarium (the hours)

Matins	12:00 midnight
Lauds	3:00 A.M.
Prime	6:00 A.M.
Terce	9:00 A.M.
Sext	12:00 noon
None	3:00 P.M.
Vespers	6:00 P.M.
Compline	9:00 P.M.

St, Osych's Day

Blasphemy! Rage drives my feet until I am almost running– disgraceful behavior!–along the red-brown track away from that...that hovel. How dare a peasant, a lowly commoner, refuse my request after I've told her God has placed his special blessing on her child?! Is it not bad enough that her husband faces eternal damnation for the taking of his own life? Lie to herself as she may about how her man died, every soul in this vale knows that it was at his own will, if not by his own hand, no matter what that newcomer to this shire declared at the inquest.

All too soon I am gasping for breath and must stop. I find a coppiced ash that yet retains most of its summer raiment, although the once vibrant green leaves are now a rusting yellow. The tree's many slender trunks offer a welcome dappled coolness against the unseasonable heat and intense sun of this autumn afternoon.

When I regain my calm, I'm surprised at how far my anger has taken me. I know these fields, they're attached to my house. Oafs, no doubt from the hamlet whose duty it is to tend our farthest-flung rows, stride along the path in my direction, bellowing out a bawdy song as they come. Most carry pruning hooks, although a few bear shepherds' crooks. Their tools suggest they're off to collect winter firewood from the nearby forest and wasteland, as is their yearly right. To a one, their feet and legs are bare, and they've shucked the top halves of their tunics and shirts until the garments hang from their belts, sleeves dangling, revealing their naked chests.

When they notice me they fall instantly silent. The ensuing quiet is broken only by the twitter of some small bird in the branches above me. As they reach the place where I stand, each man tugs at his forelock in deference to my estate. Only two are bold enough to let their gazes meet mine.

I watch them until they are tiny figures, threading their way into a distant stand of trees. Only when they disappear does my mood steady, balancing like a scale. As it does, my faith is restored.

Fie on me! Our Holy Father would never place His blessing on this child if He meant to keep her from me, and Him. Thus, it can only be His will that her mother presently refuses. I breathe out in understanding. This child is younger than any of the others He has shown me. I must be patient.

Again I chide myself, this time for arrogance. This is another test on His part; He again seeks proof of my obedience to His will.

Content, I step out onto the path and make my way home.

Sir Alain, sheriff of this shire, slid his arm under the woman sleeping next to him. Agnes of Stanrudde sighed, her eyes opening, then smiled up at him. His heart twisted in both pleasure and pain as her plain face came to life with the love she yet bore him despite what he'd done to her.

"Good morrow, my love," she whispered, shifting until she could rest her chin on his chest. Her dark eyes glowed as her smile widened. "It is a miracle."

"What is?" he asked, wanting nothing more than to keep her close to him for all time. So it had been since they'd first lain together, more than a score of years ago, and so it would always be. The contentment he felt now made him wonder how accruing wealth and influence had ever become more valuable to him than keeping her at his side.

"That I should once more be in your bed, speaking these simple words to you," she replied, still smiling.

There was no condemnation or regret, not even the merest hint of chiding in her expression. That was Aggie. She had never expected more than he could give her. Indeed, he was far more likely than she to rage against the perfidies of fate and rank that had conspired to prevent a more perfect union between them.

"And here you shall remain until the end of my days." He made his words a vow, the only vow he was free to give her.

She frowned at that. "How can that be? I thought—"

"He is dead. I heard at the Michaelmas court. My bitch of a wife is now without kith or kin to fight her battles for her. And if she doesn't care for how I live my life, she can seek out a convent to give her shelter." He freed a harsh breath at that thought. "Pity the poor abbess who agrees to take her, along with her ill temper and unending complaints."

"Ah." Aggie's smile curved in understanding. "That is why you came for me, and that is why we are at Aldersby."

"Would that I had come sooner. If only I'd known—" Alain began.

She pressed a stilling finger to his lips, forestalling his excuses and apologies. "It matters not. You came, and here I am, just where I have always longed to be."

Then, lowering her hand, she studied him, pleasure

dying to something more sober in her gaze. "But you do know you cannot keep me here, aye?"

"I will keep you where I please," Alain retorted, frowning at her, hoping that her brief marriage hadn't changed her. Aggie had never before volunteered comments or opinions, despite the sharp intelligence that had originally drawn him to her.

She shook her head. "I cannot—*will* not stay here, not when doing so is certain to bring about your destruction," she whispered, then pushed herself upright until she sat on the mattress next to him.

Her rejection drove him up as well until he was seated at her side. "My destruction? What nonsense. I told you. There's no one left to keep us apart," he laughed, hiding his irritation at her boldness.

"Oh, but there is," she replied, her gaze yet steadily meeting his. "He knows. Even if he did not challenge you as you expected, he knows. Trust me. He'll be watching for his opportunity, waiting for his chance to exploit it. My love, I will not be the cause of your destruction. You must hide me well."

Her refusal tore through him, doing almost as much injury as the insult couched in her words. "That cowardly boy?" he mocked.

She made a soothing sound and shifted closer until she was again pressed to him. Despite his irritation with her, he couldn't stop himself from embracing her. He needed to feel the beat of her heart against his own.

"You know better, love," she murmured. "I will not stay here, knowing that you use me to hurt your wife and knowing, as you do as well, that she will be looking for a new champion to fight her battles for her. Find a cottage in some hamlet near Killingworth that I may use as my own, then visit me sparingly, doing so for your safety and the sake of my heart."

Alain swallowed his irritable reaction. Aggie was only trying to protect him, just as she has always done, even if what she requested resulted in her own pain.

Alain's eyes narrowed. As long as he was sheriff here, this shire was his to rule. Those who were loyal to him would remain loyal, and would do what he required. No matter what Aggie said, he knew that puling knight, that ragtag poor relation of a man Alain had once considered a friend, lacked the courage and honor to fight his own battles. As soon as he was dispatched, Alain would see to it that any new *Coronarii* elected in this shire were men he could trust.

Chapter One

"I will not do it," Brother Edmund protested, nay, pronounced, his well-made face twisting in disgust. Then he blinked rapidly, a sign that he realized just how rude his response had been. "What I mean, sir, is that I cannot do it. That is a woman," he amended, pointing the feathery end of his ink-stained quill at the corpse in the corner of this November-chilled chamber.

Sir Faucon de Ramis, the newly-elected *Coronarius* for this shire and now proud master of Blacklea Village, sent a narrow-eyed look at his clerk. He and Edmund had known each other for all of two sennights, the same amount of time that Faucon had been responsible for keeping the shire's pleas. Although that had been long enough for him to discover much good in Edmund, his clerk daily tested the limits of his patience.

Two weeks had also been enough time for Faucon to learn that Edmund could use an excuse as well as any other man, be he knight, cleric or commoner. While it was true that the Benedictine brothers were avowed not to touch women, both he and Edmund knew that wasn't why the monk was resisting his master's command. Edmund no more wanted to expose himself to the possibility of fleas than did Faucon.

Edmund met Faucon's gaze in a wide-eyed pretense of innocence. Then he cleared his throat. Faucon now knew that sign, too. Edmund meant to resist his command with all his might.

A low rumble of amusement rose from the seven men and three women crowded into this impoverished chamber. Although Faucon and Edmund were speaking in their native French while the watching commoners spoke only English, these folk were hardly strangers to the covert war presently being waged between master and servant. This was the sort of battle they prosecuted daily, resisting their own rightful masters. So it had always been between those who were born to serve and those whose God-given right it was to command service.

"What I mean, sir," Edmund amended, "is that I cannot assist you, not if I'm also to record the names of all these witnesses prior to you calling the inquest."

This time, the clerk used the end of his quill to indicate the watching folk. As he did, the wide sleeve of his black habit swept across the surface of the parchment on his lap desk. Edmund, who intended precision and perfection in all things at all times, squeaked in dismay.

"Nay! I've smeared the ink! Now I shall have to scrape all off and begin again."

All else forgotten, the monk retrieved his knife from the lidded basket in which he transported his scribing tools, and began to hone its edge on his stone. Faucon grimaced in defeat. How much easier it was to force a man to his will when armed with a sword rather than just his tongue.

Pivoting, he aimed the full force of his frustration at the corpse as if he could blame her for setting him on yet another fool's errand. His new position as Coronarius had been created out of whole cloth at the Michaelmas court a little more than a month ago. The unstated purpose of the position was to insure more of this shire's pennies made their way into the Lionheart's strongboxes, and less into the purse of Sir Alain, this shire's sheriff.

So far, Faucon had failed miserably at his purpose. Of the six deaths, two burglaries and one rape, which had turned out to be a lover's spat, that Edmund had recorded onto their ever-lengthening roll of parchment, not one event had added so much as a farthing of profit to the king's treasure chests. If Faucon wished to reward his uncle's faith in him, then he needed a death where the murderer had at least some wealth to his name that could be confiscated in the king's name.

That most certainly didn't describe Garret of Stanrudde. Both Garret and his dead mother were but day laborers, working as weavers of linen cloth, or so said the half-finished pieces of fabric in the tall looms standing on the street wall of the chamber. The only things of value these two owned—if they owned them—were the chamber pot in the corner and the clothing hanging from the pegs near the door, which was naught but a leather curtain. No doubt even the fleas infesting both the mattress and the tattered blanket atop the corpse belonged to their landlord, the Abbey of St. Michael.

And therein lay Faucon's conundrum. With him so new to his position and this shire, it was a miracle that Abbot Athelard had known to send for him rather than the sheriff. Faucon supposed fleas and yet one more failure were a small price to pay to secure a crumb of favor with an influential abbot. Moreover, making the abbot into an ally would surely tweak Sir Alain. It was the thought of the unfinished business between him and the sheriff that ultimately propelled Faucon across the chamber.

He dropped to one knee at the edge of the mattress, which was barely more than a hen's nest contained in a worn hempen sack. Shifting his sword until it rested easily on the wooden floor, he threw back the edges of his better, vair-lined mantle, then brushed the front of his borrowed green tunic as if it were already infested with the nasty little bloodsuckers. If he did take on fleas, he'd owe an apology to Blacklea's former steward when he returned the garment, something that wouldn't happen until his own garments and personal possessions finally arrived at Blacklea. It was anyone's guess when that might happen. According to the last message from his family, his belongings were now in the custody of a wool merchant, who would pass by Blacklea as he made his way from fair to fair across the shire.

When Faucon could procrastinate no longer, he leaned gingerly forward and studied the old woman. Frail and thin, Elsa of Stanrudde lay trapped in the ever-disconcerting stillness given to the dead. Her earthly remains had already grown stiff. It had taken a good while for Faucon to reach Stanrudde from his new home. Given that the sun was well past its zenith–the bells for the hour of None had recently sounded–she must have passed sometime last night, no doubt earlier than later. Fading bruises marked her right eye socket and her left cheek.

"When you are finished plying your knife, Brother Edmund," Faucon said without turning his head and yet speaking in his mother tongue, "you must add that the dead woman shows signs of having been beaten by someone using his fists but that the bruises are days old and well on the way to healing."

He pulled back the thin blanket. As with most folk who owned but one set of clothing, the old woman had retired for the night in nothing but her wrinkled skin. Even older bruises, also the size and shape of a man's fist and an ugly shade of yellow, marked her breastbone.

Elsa's granddaughter, Ida by name, came to kneel beside Faucon. It was she who had raised the hue and cry after arriving early this morn for a visit and finding her grandmother dead; it had also been she who made the charge of murder and brought it to her kinswoman's landlord. A fair young thing, Ida wore a pair of tightly-woven gowns, the upper one bright blue, the inner one dark red. Their quality suggested she lived a better life than her grandmother and uncle.

Tears sparkled in her pale eyes as she looked at the marks that discolored her grandmother's chest. "If only my husband would have allowed me to take her into our home, but we just couldn't afford to feed another mouth," she whispered in English, her words fading into silence.

Faucon made no reply, only traced his fingers across the line of the dead woman's collarbone. Beaten but not broken. Then he rolled Elsa onto her left side. What little long gray hair remained to her streamed across the bluish-red discoloration that stained her back from shoulders to rump, save where her body had touched the pallet. That teased a grief-stricken moan from her granddaughter.

As Faucon lowered the corpse back onto the mattress, Ida leapt to her feet and pointed at her uncle. "Didn't I say that you killed her! You finally beat her to death just as I knew you would! How could you do that to your own mother?" she demanded in righteous accusation.

Panic twisted Garret of Stanrudde's features. Ida's uncle stood as far as he could from the mattress and his mother, beside the looms that paid their meager wages. Although it was mid-afternoon, Garret yet wore only his shirt and braies, the length of cloth all men wrapped around their hips to cover their nether parts. The fabric of his undergarments was ragged with age and use. As small and frail as his mother, Garret's pronounced cheekbones suggested he ate more sparingly than most monks.

"I didn't kill her!" he protested. "Didn't we both find her this morning when you came and woke me?

She was just as she is now—blue and lifeless. I told you, she was quiet all day yesterday, barely able to ply her shuttle and finishing only half as much as she usual wove. I let her be when she said she felt ill and retired early."

Still pleading, Garret turned to look at his neighbors, who had responded to his niece's calls of murder and who by law were trapped here until Faucon released them. Garret reached out to grab the man closest to him by the sleeve of his brown tunic.

"Watt, tell Sir Crowner," he pleaded, using the commoners' corruption of Faucon's Latin title, one Faucon had begun to encourage simply because he liked the sound of it. "Tell the knight that you heard no cry or complaint from her last night. Not last night!"

Watt was squat and short. Although his face was half-concealed by a wild red beard, there was no missing the dislike he felt for his neighbor. The other witnesses all shifted uneasily. Faucon recognized the meaning in their collective movement, having seen it more than once over the past weeks. Those living closest to Garret disliked him and were wondering if they might rid themselves of an irksome neighbor through simple silence or a lie of omission.

Garret saw the same thing. "Nay!" the weaver shouted. "You won't do this to me. You have to tell Sir Crowner you heard nothing, because that is the truth. You heard nothing!"

He took a step toward Faucon, his brows lifted and his arms spread wide in a gesture of innocence. "Sir, they hold their tongues because they don't like me. They would have heard her cries if I'd touched her last night. They always did. Didn't Father Herebert always come a-knocking each and every day after we fought, ready to remind me that I must honor my mother even though she had a vicious tongue and rained nothing but complaints down upon my head?"

"And no doubt your priest also reminded you that Church law doesn't allow you to beat your family with your fists, only with a stick no wider than your thumb," Brother Edmund chided under his breath and in his native tongue, his head yet bent over his parchment as he scraped off smeared ink.

Elsa's son spoke over the muttered comment. "It's not my fault that I beat her. She drove me to it, she did. But I never touched her last night. Not last night." His last words were almost a sob.

"Did you hear them arguing last night?" Faucon asked directly of his witnesses, shifting into their guttural English. He'd learned the tongue as a babe at his nurse's breast.

Once again the assembled folk shifted uneasily, this time glancing between themselves. A woman, one who looked as worn and old as Elsa although far more neatly kept in her faded orange and yellow attire, spoke up.

"Nay, it is as Garret says. All was quiet in here for a change, thank the Lord. I live right there." She pointed to the wall behind Garret's and Elsa's shared mattress. "The panel between our chambers is no thicker than this." Now she touched the neatly mended white cloth that covered her grizzled hair and pronounced her at least once married, although her words suggested her life was presently a solitary one. "I heard every word they ever said to each other. There wasn't so much as a squabble last night."

The old woman was right about the thin walls of this structure. Didn't Faucon's bones rattle in time to the rhythmic metallic ring of hammer on metal from the next door copper smithy? The pigeons loitering atop the mossy thatch roof above him could have been perched on his shoulders, so audible were their gentle coos. And, although these chambers were a full storey over the lane below, he could hear the squeak of the wheeled cart used by a costermonger hawking 'best for cider' apples, which, if Faucon's guess were correct, meant halfway to rotten. From a distance came the indistinct echoes of a good number of people screaming and shouting.

"Magda," hissed the red-bearded man.

The old woman glanced ruefully at her neighbors. "I cannot lie, not about this, not when I must forever after carry it upon my soul," she whispered, her tone begging their forgiveness for her forward speech. It was not a woman's place to give such testimony.

The tallest of the men, who wore an oft-repaired green tunic sighed. "Nor should you," he agreed, although his expression suggested he regretted her honesty. He put his arm around the woman next to him, who was nearly as tall as he, then looked at Faucon. "Magda is right. Neither my wife nor I heard anything from them yesterday. We noted it because it was unusual for them not to at least bicker."

Faucon expected no other answer, but Elsa's granddaughter moaned in disappointment. "But he beat her all the time. You can see the bruises. Look at her back! It's nothing but a great bruise," she insisted.

Once again brushing hopefully at his tunic—as if something so simple as a flick of his wrist could actually dislodge any of the fleas that might have found him—Faucon came to his feet. He shook his head to deny her charge. "That is not bruising and well you know it, goodwife," he told her gently.

There wasn't a soul in this world who hadn't helped wash or wrap a dead kinsman in preparation for burial. If even the smallest children knew such coloring was a natural process that affected all the dead, no matter the cause of their demise, then Ida did as well. He suspected her own guilt was keeping her from admitting it.

"Your grandmother clearly passed in her sleep. At her age, her death can hardly be considered sudden, nor was it homicide or a death felonious," he added, using the term that legally described the mortal sin of suicide. "Against that, there is no point in calling for an inquest, not when the only possible verdict is that our Lord's angels came to bear your grandmother's soul away with them."

"God bless you, sir!" Garret cried, his voice rising almost to falsetto in his relief as he staggered back to collide with his loom. It clattered as it shifted.

At the same instant, the apple seller in the lane broke off mid-cry to shriek, "Stop, you! Vandal! You've broken my cart and spilled my apples!"

"Grab him, you! Don't let him pass! Murderer!" another man screamed.

A third offered a gasping, "Neighbors, stop him, stop Peter, son of Roger! He's killed Bernart the Linsman!"

Chapter Two

"Stay here!" Faucon commanded of everyone in the room as he thrust through his witnesses in response to the hue and cry.

Shoving back the leather door flap, he half-leapt, half-clattered down the narrow wooden stairs—hardly more than a short ladder—that led to the coppersmith's storage room at street level. Yanking open the storeroom door, he shot out into the narrow lane.

And was instantly swept into a panting, boiling throng of racing townsmen. Like water around a rock, these men, and they were male to a one, surged around the costermonger, who was draped protectively over his toppled apple cart and what remained of his wares.

Running alongside a butcher in his blood-stained leather apron, Faucon ducked under a house's low-hanging second storey, which jettied out halfway over the lane. The mob bore left onto another lane, even more narrow than the first. It was coopers and carpenters here, or so said the barrels set out in display and the tools held by the workmen gawking from the wide openings in the streetside walls of their home workshops.

This lane ended at the steps of an ancient stone church roofed in slate. It was a tiny structure, as was common for sanctuaries of its age, but not forgotten. Its newest parishioners had been generous with their tithes; a half-built square stone tower covered the apse end of their church.

An elderly priest with a wild mane of silver hair stood upon the raised porch before the metal-bound door to his church. Of medium height but slight in build, in one hand he carried the shepherd's crook that symbolized his authority to lead his flock. Like Moses before the sea, he spread his arms. Beneath his cloak, the wide sleeves of his cassock trailed down from his arms, looking like angel wings.

If he meant to forestall the mob from climbing the three steps and entering the church, he succeeded. Men ebbed back from the steps, stumbling into those yet rushing forward. A great roar of frustration filled the air as the hue and cry went this way and that, Faucon among them.

Some, like he, ended up pressed against the walls of the shops and stalls which lined the square. The youngest among these—apprentices dressed in the overly large tunics and sagging chausses that were the mark of their position, no matter their trade—as well as the most agile men swiftly sought refuge from the press by climbing the sides of the two-storey dwellings to roost like the pigeons on their thatched roofs.

Faucon braced himself against the edge of the lower horizontal shutter on the coffermaker's shop window. The dozen or so tiny wooden boxes displayed on it rattled. Then, pressing forward, he put his shoulder to the pair of tanners' lads who blocked his path. Burly boys both, they reeked of rotten meat and the oaken acid that turned animal skin into leather.

They turned on him with snarls and clenched fists. Faucon lifted his chin. His broad brow and long nose wore the stamp of his uncle's aristocratic family, and his black hair and beard marked him as among those Normans who ruled this country. Then, to be certain the lads completely understood him, he pushed the edge of his mantle over his shoulder so they could see both his weapon and the silver that chased his sword belt and its sheath. Eyes wide, they opened their hands and fell back, knocking into others who growled with equal displeasure. And so it went, man by man, as Faucon pushed his way steadily toward the church.

"You will give him to us, Father Herebert!" came a commanding bellow from the far end of the crowd, where the lane entered the small square formed by church and shops.

Faucon craned his neck wondering who was foolish enough to think he could demand compliance from a priest. In this case, the fool was a heavy-set man, albeit tall and handsome. He wore a closely-trimmed brown beard while his hair, the same dark color, fell to his shoulders, as was the present fashion, one that Faucon also followed.

The leather apron he wore atop his orange tunic said the man was a merchant. while the yellowed blotches where the bright color had been leached from his garment suggested he was a pleykster, the tradesman who bleached linen and newly-spun wool so it might better take on the dyers' hues. Standing alongside the pleykster were three young men dressed in identical green woolen tunics decorated with the town's emblem. Each wore a common soldier's short sword, naming them members of the town guard.

Yet huffing after the exertion of the chase, the pleykster raised a fist. "We, not you, will hold Peter until our sheriff comes," he panted out. "You will not keep him from us, not when I need to make him pay for slaughtering the man who was my friend, a man who would soon have been his father-by-marriage!"

The announcement of such a betrayal made the men in the lane roar anew, even though most must have already known who this Peter was and how he was connected to his victim. The angry sound echoed like thunder in the confined space.

With the guardsmen to carve a path for him, the big

man strode easily through the crowd, reaching the church steps well ahead of Faucon. He mounted the lowest step so that he could be seen by everyone in the square. That brought him almost eye-to-eye with the priest. His fists closed in threat.

"Now open your door, Father Herebert, and give us Peter, son of Roger the Webber!" the big man demanded of the clergyman.

"You shall not have him, Hodge," Father Herebert returned calmly. Well-honed after chanting countless masses, his deep voice carried easily to every corner of the square. He paused to glance across the faces of his parishioners. "Peter now sits in our frith stool. As Church law and our ancient traditions require, I have granted him his forty days of sanctuary."

Only a few groans of disappointment rose from the crowd at this. The priest's announcement was no more than Faucon and any other man here expected. A clergyman's authority in the matter of sanctuary was absolute, and what had been granted could not be retracted.

Having vented their rage during the chase, the watching men and boys now settled into an uneasy quiet, their attention on the pleykster as they waited to see what the man might next do. They should have been watching their new crowner.

Although Faucon was too late–or, more rightly, too early–to take custody of the murderer, forty days left him plenty of time to put his hand about the murderer's estate. To achieve that, he'd need the cooperation of all these men. This time, when he set his shoulder to the men in front of him, he shouted in his native tongue, "Move aside! Make way for a servant of the crown!"

Startled, those in front of him did as he commanded, while in every corner of this crowded square men shifted to see the newcomer who spoke the Norman tongue and claimed such an august, if unknown, role. On the porch, Father Herebert lowered his arms and leaned heavily on his crook. Relief softened the old man's round face as he noted Faucon's expensive weapon and recognized in it the possibility of a knight's support, if not rescue.

As Faucon stopped on the cobbled apron at the base of the church steps, the clergyman, speaking for all of Stanrudde, demanded, "Who comes?"

"Sir Faucon de Ramis, master of Blacklea Village and newly-elected Coronarius for this shire," Faucon replied, offering the priest the show of humility due his station.

From his stance on the lowest step, Hodge the Pleykster studied Faucon with narrowed eyes. Subtle dislike tainted the merchant's well-made features. Such a reaction was hardly unusual among those who earned their coins by the sweat of their brows. More than a few resented their betters, who dared claim a portion of their profits by right of birth alone. Faucon eyed him in return. The pleykster must have come directly from his pots to join the chase. His tunic was damp and reeked of urine, one of the substances he used in his trade.

"A servant of the crown, are you?" the priest challenged. "Tell me, sir. How is it that you intend to serve the crown in this instance? Charges of murder belong to our sheriff and matters of sanctuary to our Lord."

"That is no longer so," Faucon started to reply.

"At the command of Archbishop Hubert Walter. It is no longer the sheriff's duty to attend to the murdered or call inquests," came Brother Edmund's frantic shout from the back of the square. "Sir Faucon, I come! Let me pass! Stand aside, I say. You will let me pass!"

Despite the command in his voice and the authority of his black habit, the men blocking Edmund's way didn't move. Raising an arm to catch his employer's attention, the clerk jumped. His basket of tools, once more strapped to his back, bounced with him, rising above his tonsured head for a brief instant before falling back between his shoulders.

Father Herebert frowned as he glanced from the stymied monk to his master. "If it is true that murderers are no longer the concern of Sir Alain, then why do I and these men," he indicated the townsmen filling in the square, "know nothing of you or your appointment, sir?"

"The position of Coronarius is new. Command them to let my clerk pass and you will have your answer. Brother Edmund carries with him proof of my right, given to me by Bishop William of Hereford," Faucon said.

After confronting this same question at every turn since taking up his duties, Faucon had parted with precious coins to send a man to Bishop William, who was his great-uncle. The uncle's private clerk, a man who was also one of Faucon's cousins, had returned the requested proof at the same swift speed.

When Father Herebert raised his hand in command, the crowd parted for Edmund. The monk pressed his elbows close to his sides, and keeping a hand curled tightly to the strap that held his basket on his back, he lowered his head and drove straight through the press, not caring whom he jostled as he passed.

Once he stood beside Faucon, he opened the leather scrip hanging from his belt and brought forth a packet wrapped in soft cloth. Folding back the fabric, he held up the parchment that testified Faucon rightfully claimed his special relationship to court and king. That parchment said nothing at all about Faucon's duties. That wasn't something that could yet be done, mostly because the archbishop hadn't specifically named his duties.

Not that anything scribed on the bit of skin mattered to any man in this crowd. Nay, what convinced them and other folk in this shire that Faucon served those who ruled this land was the large red wax disk that hung by threads sewn to the edge of the parchment. On its face was the imprint of the bishop's seal.

Edmund climbed the steps to offer their proof to the priest. Father Herebert took the parchment and wax disk, holding it aloft for all to see. Faucon climbed to stand on the step above the pleykster and faced the men in the square. To a one, they watched him in return.

"At the Michaelmas court just past, our Archbishop of Canterbury did decree that Sir Alain will no longer keep the pleas of this shire or call your inquest juries," Faucon told them, his voice raised to reach every corner. Then he hesitated and drew a bracing breath.

"Thus, it is now my duty in this shire to investigate all murders and other unnatural deaths, and my responsibility to determine who did the deed so I may confiscate the king's portion of the wrongdoer's estate, as the law allows."

That wasn't precisely a lie, but it was a dodge, one that Faucon daily became more adept at offering. Even he thought it far more likely that the archbishop intended his new Coronarii to do no more than make note who died and how they passed, as well as noting any fees or fines to be collected from the wrongdoer. But to Faucon's way of thinking, if the king wished to profit from the estates of those who committed murder, then someone had to deduce whose property needed to be attached. And in this shire, that someone was going to be him.

The priest moved his jaw as if he chewed on this information and found it unpalatable. Faucon continued, giving the clergyman no chance to question or pry.

"If you doubt the proof that we have presented here, call for Abbot Athelard. It is at his behest that I am presently in Stanrudde. He sent for me so I might investigate the death of one of his tenants."

"This is true," Brother Edmund seconded as both he and Faucon retreated down the steps. Having retrieved their precious seal and parchment from the priest, Edmund came to a halt directly beside Faucon rather than slightly behind his master as was proper for a servant. After tucking their proof back into his scrip, he looked up at the priest. "At the command of Archbishop Hubert Walter you must cede all authority in the matter of the linsman's death to Sir Faucon. He, and only he, will arrest the one who did this deed."

As always, Edmund's natural arrogance ran roughshod over the good he intended. The old priest's eyes narrowed. He freed a harsh sound.

"I care nothing for the duties you claim or your authority to claim them, or even the authority of our archbishop in this matter," he shouted out, announcing his defiance to all who could hear him. "They are matters belonging to the world of Man. I have granted Peter the Webber sanctuary. No one, not you"—he lifted his crook and swept its base forward until he pointed at the three men of the guard who stood on the far side of the steps, "nor you"—the tip now aimed at Hodge the Pleykster—"nor you"—he pointed the crook at Faucon—"has the right to remove him from these walls. Not even the sheriff's men speaking in our king's name can do this."

"That is as you say, Father," Faucon agreed with a smile, trying to soothe where Edmund had injured. "But you and I both know that forty days hence this man Peter must exit your church. On that day I will be here, ready to take his confession."

"Or, if he will not confess his crime," Edmund interjected, "then Sir Faucon will command him to abjure our realm. He will be driven from home and hearth for all time, with no hope of returning to our shores."

As determined as the crowd had been to prevent Peter the Webber from claiming sanctuary in this holy place, to a one they groaned at the idea of his banishment. It was a rare man who didn't tremble at the thought of being stripped of all that was familiar to be sent to where folk knew him not. Faucon understood their reaction. He'd been a crusader with the Lionheart, and had spent far longer than he liked traveling through foreign lands fraught with strange tongues and odd customs.

Father Herebert once more leaned heavily on his crook. "So it has always been, sir. Come you for him in forty days, for you cannot have him now."

With that, he turned and limped back into the world he ruled. When he closed the church door behind him, Faucon heard the bar drop into its brackets. It was a symbolic gesture. Within a quarter hour the church door would be under guard by the town's defenders. The door would remain watched for every moment of the next weeks to prevent Peter the Webber from escaping both the church and his rightful punishment.

Nor was the guard the only thing that would hold the webber close over the next long, lonely weeks. For, if Peter wanted to remain in his sanctuary, he could not leave the frith stool. Now there was a truly terrifying thought, being imprisoned in a stone chair for every moment of the day. Every person who entered the church, whether to attend a daily mass, a baptism or a funeral, would watch him. Should Peter lose physical contact with that chair even for an instant, even while relieving himself, his right to sanctuary would end. Anyone who witnessed that moment could fall upon him and drag him from the church to face his fate.

Hodge stepped off the stair, halting beside Faucon although he yet faced the men of the hue and cry. "Aye, sanctuary Peter, son of Roger, has for the now, but I am a patient man. In forty days I will be here to see that he pays for what he has done to my friend and yours!" he shouted.

The crowd roared their agreement. Faucon wondered whom these men liked so well, the pleykster or the dead linen merchant.

Edmund grabbed Faucon by the arm. His gaze was frantic. "They're all going to leave now but they cannot, not when I must scribe the name of the one who raised the hue and cry. They can't go until I know it!"

Faucon shot him an irritable look. "Why are you even here? Did I not command you to stay?"

Edmund blinked in astonishment at that. "Surely, you didn't intend that command for me. You need me."

With that, he released his master to race up the steps to the porch. "Stay, all of you! You cannot leave yet," he shouted. "Sir Crowner and I must know who found the body. Who raised the hue and cry? And we must have proof of Englishry!"

It was enough to make Faucon's head ache. Edmund was right; these bits of information were what they needed to record. But this was neither the place to do it nor the right way to achieve the townsmen's cooperation.

"Edmund, come down," he commanded without heat. "What eats at you that you've forgotten the proper order of things? Isn't our first task to view the body?"

Edmund aimed a horrified look at his master. "Lord save me! What have I done?" he breathed out, his face ashen.

Hodge the Pleykster glanced from monk to master. "It was Bernart's wife, God pity her, who found Bernart. She saw Peter yet crouching beside my friend, his hands stained with her husband's blood."

Now that the confrontation had ended, the big man's voice had lost its angry edge. His expression sagged with exhaustion and grief. He more fell than sat onto the middle step. His gaze aimed at the cobbled earth beneath his feet, he shook his head like one stunned. "To think I ever felt any fondness for that cowardly murdering boy," he muttered.

One of the guardsmen stepped around the grieving merchant. Like his mates, he appeared no older than the four-and-twenty years Faucon claimed. His sword was serviceable, its belt and sheath made of sturdy leather, but he wore a leather cap instead of a metal helmet. This was no professional soldier. Nay, if Stanrudde was like any of the towns Faucon knew, this man was a journeyman in one of the local trades. Just as the great barons were only required to lend their swords and soldiers to the king for forty days each year, so did each town require their merchants to provide men to train as soldiers for a similar period so their city's walls might be protected all the year round at no expense.

"Is it really true that we no longer need to call for Sir Alain in this matter?" the guardsman asked, his brows raised even as he lowered his head as if to conceal his conversation from the pleykster.

"It is," Faucon assured him.

The young man gave an approving nod. It wasn't the first time Faucon had witnessed satisfaction at this change in the sheriff's authority. Although Sir Alain yet had his hand well fastened around the throat of this shire, he was not well liked, at least not by the meanest of its citizenry.

When the soldier continued, he lowered his voice until he was almost whispering. "Then you must come with me to Bernart le Linsman's home. You must do more than simply view the merchant's body and call the inquest. You must discern what truly happened, for I and my companions," the jerk of his head indicated the other two guardsmen, "know in our souls that Peter did not do this deed."

Chapter Three

"**I** cannot believe I so completely lost my head! Indeed, you were correct, sir," Edmund muttered, his head bowed as if he were shamed. He and Faucon were following the guardsmen out of the square, returning along the same path they'd run with the hue and cry.

Faucon glanced at his clerk and restrained a laugh. It wouldn't do to mock Edmund for an apology, not when it was the first one his clerk had offered in their short acquaintance. Although Edmund hadn't yet confirmed this, Faucon guessed it was the monk's resistance to admitting error that had cost him his convent home and resulted in his demotion to a mere Crowner's clerk.

Still, he couldn't resist asking, "I am right about what?"

The monk shot him a quick glance, then once more focused his gaze on the rutted earthen lane beneath his sandals. "That our first order of business is always to see the body. If we have not determined how the death occurred, then we cannot know how to proceed, can we?"

Edmund fell silent for a few more steps, then began again to mutter. "It must have been the excitement of the chase that addled me. Of course, that's what it must have been. Untoward excitement on my part."

"Sir Crowner?" Now fully dressed, Garret, son of Elsa, lifted his hand to capture Faucon's attention. He stood in the storeroom doorway below the chamber that was his home. "Sir, I know you bade us wait, but it appears you have other business at hand now. Am I free to have my mother's body washed and prepared for burial, and can my neighbors go on about what's left of their day?"

"Aye," Faucon told him.

"Nay!" Edmund called over him.

Faucon's jaw set. He caught his clerk by the sleeve and dragged him to a halt. Edmund squeaked in surprise and yanked on his trapped arm; he wasn't a man who much enjoyed human contact. The guardsmen stopped with them, watching in untoward curiosity.

"Brother Edmund, by what right do you countermand my order?" Faucon demanded quietly. "I told Mistress Ida that I would not call an inquest jury in the matter of her grandmother's death."

Edmund frowned at him, still shifting uneasily as he tried more surreptitiously to free his arm. "Aye, so you did tell the granddaughter, but you had no right to offer her what you did. Once the charge of murder has been made you must call the inquest jury and instruct them to either confirm or deny the charge. But, before I could inform you that you had misspoken, you were gone as part of the hue and cry.

"Sir, we truly have no choice. It is the law," the monk added, almost pleading. "As you have just reminded me, all things have their proper order."

It took every ounce of Faucon's will not to draw his sword and end his torment by either murder or death felonious. Unfortunately, murder wasn't an option, not when he owed Edmund his life. Nor was Faucon ready to pursue death felonious. This wasn't because killing himself assured his eternal damnation. Nay, he wasn't leaving this earthly vale until he'd wrung every last drop of pleasure from his new home and the unexpected income that came with it. But God take him, this time

Edmund would bend!

"I will not call the inquest jury for this death," he warned the monk. "I have deemed that the old woman died in her sleep. There was no murder and there is no profit to the crown in pursuing the matter further. You may note in your record that I said as much, even if what you scribe results in my being fined by king and court for not doing my duty or breaking the law."

Edmund's eyes grew hollow as he contemplated his master so flagrantly violating the rules that structured his every breath. An instant later, his shoulders relaxed. "Aye, sir, I can see your point. But consider this. I've already recorded the names of the witnesses and the victim. Now, here we are with a new death to record, one we know for certain is murder and nothing else. When you call the inquest to confirm the verdict for the linsman, why not have them also deny the verdict of murder for Elsa of Stanrudde, confirming instead one of natural death?" New excitement filled the clerk's dark eyes as if he'd both surprised and pleased himself with his suggestion.

Faucon frowned at the monk. Was Edmund haggling with him? Well, he could haggle as well as the next man, and he was going to get what he wanted.

"So we can do, but it's already past None. The sun will be setting around Vespers tonight, giving us no more than another two hours or so to call the jury for the murdered linsman. If we aren't able to do it by then, I won't prevent Elsa of Stanrudde from being buried on the morrow, as is her right."

Much to Faucon's surprise, Edmund merely shrugged. "But if we do call the jury before day's end, she'll yet be available for viewing. If not, well then, we can exhume her when the time comes and present her for the jurors to view," he replied in what sounded to Faucon like casual satisfaction, something he hadn't believe Edmund capable of.

Then, as Faucon watched in astonishment, the monk's lips shifted until they were bent into the oddest, flattest smile he had ever seen, and the first that Edmund had offered him. The expression was so startling that all Faucon could do was stare.

When his master said nothing, Edmund's strange grin faltered. "Will that not suffice, sir?" he prodded hopefully. "Both the law and your dictate will be satisfied, no? And you'll have no need to worry over fines and fees for doing wrong on your part."

And that made Faucon gape like an oaf. Edmund was bending on this to protect his master from a fine? Faucon wasn't certain if he wanted to thank his clerk or beat his brow against the nearest wooden beam. At last, all he could think to do was smile in return. "Aye, Brother Edmund, that will do well, indeed. My thanks."

The clerk nodded. The unusual lights dimmed from his gaze and his expression once more regained its usual disapproving bend. "I am glad I could clarify for you, sir."

Wanting to shake his head like one stunned, Faucon turned to look at the weaver. "If I do not call you to bring your mother to an inquest before the sun sets this night, you may bury your mother on the morrow in all peace, goodman, taking with you my condolences on your loss."

As with most towns and even the great city of London, Stanrudde's streets were a twisting warren of narrow lanes, some no wider than a man was tall. As Faucon rounded each turn, his respect for Peter the Webber's fleetness of foot grew. The man's path had taken him through places so constricted that he could have been stopped if someone on either side of the lane had simply stretched out his arm.

Here in the parish where the middling craftsmen and day laborers plied their trades, the houses were older and more worn, hogs and chickens wandering where they would. All of the structures sat cheek by jowl, the exterior walls of each home almost touching those of its neighbors. To a one, these dwellings were painted white and built of wattle and daub—branches woven into panels and coated with mud and manure—reinforced with dark wooden cross bracing. Most rose no higher than two storeys, although a rare few pressed their thatched roofs to the sky at three.

Just now, every window in those upper storeys was open, every shutter thrown wide. Women and old men, little lads and girls, crowded the openings. While the children laughed and tossed playthings back and forth across the lanes, their elders leaned out as far as possible, chattering and shouting to one another as they shared their excitement over Bernart le Linsman's murder and Peter the Webber's race for sanctuary.

As the guard led them around another corner, Faucon caught a delicious note in the general stench of so many lives lived so closely. He dared a deep breath, then savored the rich fragrance of fermenting ale and the more subtle aroma of stewing lamb. An alewife's home, and one worthy of her trade if those smells bore good witness. He marked the structure in his mind. Should he and Edmund be barred into the city for the night, Edmund was guaranteed a bed with his brethren at the abbey, but Faucon would need a place to lay his head if the abbot refused him the abbey's guesthouse. Alewives often set aside a corner for travelers.

Their final turn took them out of the crowded city center and into a new world, one inhabited by the town's most successful merchants. These were the men who ruled Stanrudde with as much power and influence as his great-uncle exercised over his bishopric and its far-flung holdings. In this area of town there were no streetside shop windows in the workshops that surely yet existed in the ground level of these grand stone houses. Nay, the merchants who lived here didn't need to entice shoppers to buy their wares by announcing to all and sundry what they sold. Instead, anyone wishing to purchase what they had in store had to prove their ability to afford it. With no need to encourage trade, these homeowners had all raised stone walls to enclose their private realms, not only to protect their expensive ware, but also their wealth in workshops, livestock, outbuildings and land that they enjoyed.

It was a simple matter to identify which of these fine homes belonged to Bernart le Linsman. Measuring more than three perches long and a full three storeys tall, and surrounded by a low enclosing wall, the house was not only the largest dwelling on this short lane, but a dozen women and girls, all wearing pale blue linen overgowns, huddled beneath the arch that marked the gateway. Most of them wept gently, but a few had torn at their hair and clothing and were still moaning loudly in their grief.

"Jeanne!" called one of the guardsmen as they drew near the mourners.

His call stirred a child of no more than ten. She broke from the group and flung herself at the soldier with a wordless cry. Burying her face in his chest, she sobbed, "I cannot believe it! How can the master be dead and Master Peter be the one who killed him?"

"My sister," the soldier offered Faucon in explanation. "She's apprenticed here to learn the art of needlework from Mistress Alina. Calm yourself, sweetling," he told his sister. "We've brought a knight, our shire's new Coro–" the soldier looked up, frowning as he sought to recall Faucon's title.

"You may call me Sir Crowner," Faucon replied, then smiled at the girl. "Come little Jeanne. My clerk and I must meet with your master's wife or your steward, if your house employs such a man. We are ordered by our king to pursue the matter of your master's death."

The child stepped away from her brother, wiping her cheeks with the backs of her hands. Although her lower lip still trembled, she offered her Crowner a quick curtsey. "We have no steward here, sir," she said, "and even if we did, all the men of the house are gone. They all raced after–" her voice broke and she drew a ragged sob, then forged on. "I fear our mistress is distraught past speaking, but come within and I'll fetch Mistress Gisla for you instead."

Turning, she hurried through the gate. Faucon followed. There was no need to beg her companions to make way for him. Upon noting the arrival of a strange man, even one accompanied by a monk, the maidservants and other female apprentices had all eased back to stand in fearful clutches against the wall as they watched him. While the guardsmen went to assure their neighbors and kinswomen as best they could, Faucon made his way into the linsman's cobbled courtyard, with Edmund close on his heels.

Like most merchants of Bernart's ilk, his home and outbuildings stood right off the lane, no doubt because that was where his ancestors had set their roots. However, his exterior wall enclosed a good deal of land. Although only a little wider than the courtyard, the end of this spacious rectangle of property couldn't be seen in the distance, not with a line of apple trees hiding the back wall. This more rural portion of the merchant's home started at the back of what must be the household's kitchen. The sizable wooden shed stood at the west end of the courtyard, directly in front of Faucon, a few chickens and ducks wandered around its edges. To one side of the kitchen, a pair of hogs, tethered to a post by thongs tied to the rings in their noses, lazed on the sun-warmed cobbles. A great iron pot stood to one side of that post, suggesting that Bernart's unexpected death had granted these creatures one more day of life.

On the northern side of the courtyard, to Faucon's right, was a slate-roofed wooden storehouse. The barn-like structure was as long as the house, but not as tall. Its door stood wide, revealing a good number of worktables on which linen fabric was spread. Some of the pieces retained the natural color of the flax from which they'd been woven, while others had been dyed in as many colors as Faucon could imagine. The shortest and most forward of the tables held several feet of fabric bleached to a stark and snowy white. This cloth was so fine that the day's breathy breeze sent it fluttering and drifting across the tabletop.

The house to the south, across from the storehouse, was everything Faucon expected. There had indeed been a ground level workshop in the structure at one time, proving that like many other of England's new men of commerce, Bernart had risen from humbler stock to his present wealth. But the usual long window that allowed passersby to view the craftsman at his work had been bricked shut. This created a slightly off-color rectangle in the house's front wall. Three windows, each about the shape and size of half a small cart wheel, had been cut into this new brick, saying that the old workshop was still used by the household. One of those windows was open, for the arched opening showed no sign of the interior wooden shutters that darkened the other two.

Gone was the small door that had once led into the workshop. More new brick filled in its former space beneath a modest arch of stone. Now folk found their way into the house through a door as grand as any king might claim for his home. Set at the exact center of the structure, it was framed by a pointed arch of decorative stone that soared high onto the house's second storey.

Beneath the arch was a massive wooden door with a great loop of iron as its door handle, complete with a slot for a key.

Faucon knew both that handle's form and its function. When the handle turned, gears on the inside of the door rotated, lowering bars into brackets to protect the house. From the outside it took a key to unlock the gears, so an opposite turn of the handle could lift the bars back into the open position.

Just now the door was both unbarred and ajar. Jeanne slipped into the narrow gap, then shoved at the heavy panel so Faucon could follow. But by the time he stepped inside, the child was nowhere to be seen.

He looked from the set of stairs directly ahead of him to the short entryway that included a small door to his left. This could only be the interior access to the workshop. Faucon choose the stairs, certain that they would lead him to the linsman's hall. It was curiosity that drove him; he wanted to see how the wealthy merchant lived.

The first set of stairs rose only a few steps before turning back on itself to go higher still, taking him to a landing with a door on either side. The door to his left was closed while the one to his right stood ajar. He touched the rightward door. With a gentle creak, it swung a little wider.

Faucon caught his breath in admiration. This chamber rivaled any he'd ever seen, including those belonging to his wealthy kinsmen. What he could see of the walls was coated in thick plaster, painted the same shade of pale blue worn by the maidservants. Four carved stone columns lined the south-facing wall. Each column was painted yellow and trimmed in a green so fresh it reminded Faucon of spring. The carved foliage decorating their capitals had been picked out in a darker green, from which the occasional red berry peeked. That berry-red hue had been used on the arching stone ribs that rose from the capitals to hold aloft the floor of the uppermost storey.

This arrangement of columns had created three substantial bays between them. A tall window was cut into the wall of each bay, each window divided into thirds by carved stonework. These stone dividers had also been painted red, as had the decorative pointed arches that framed the windows.

Rather than the fabulously expensive glass Faucon had seen in some churches while he traveled the world, the linsman had filled his windows with his own product. Fine linen cloth, surely either greased or waxed to stave off the elements, had been stretched tightly in the openings. Although this did nothing to stop the chill air from entering, the sun flowed through almost undaunted. Today, that was light enough to tease glints of gold from the dried rushes strewn across the wide wooden planks in the floor.

Each bay held three wooden benches, one on each side of the bay. Stored beneath these seats were baskets of all shapes and sizes. Threads in as many colors as the rainbow trailed from each of these woven containers. Stacked carefully atop the benches were dozens of wooden frames, both square and circular. Stretched within each frame were narrow lengths of linen onto which a colorful repeating pattern was being embroidered. It took Faucon a moment to realize these cloth strips would soon be ribbons, trim for the hems and necklines of gowns or tunics. He even owned several garments decorated with this sort of ribbon, but he hadn't purchased that work. Instead, it had been done by his mother's maids.

Three standing frames, each as tall as a man, were aligned with the openings of each bay, their placement calculated so that sunlight would illuminate them for the greater part of the day. Piled on either side of these frames were soft folds of fabric as wide as the frame and the loom that had woven it. On one side of the frame, the cloth was yet undecorated. By the time it had been folded into the pile on the opposite side of the frame, the needlewomen who labored in this house had added a colorful and intricate design.

Bernart of Stanrudde wasn't the usual sort of linsman, the merchant who sold coifs and braies or the occasional shirt made of that fabric. Nor would the folk of Stanrudde ever wear garments made in his house. Nay, these fabrics were the sort purchased by earls and princes.

"It is easier to thread a rope through the eye of a needle than for a rich man to enter heaven," Edmund muttered. Every line of his body radiated disapproval.

"Perhaps," Faucon replied, wondering just how much it might cost to purchase a tunic made from Bernart's work, "but you cannot deny that this is a beautiful chamber."

Edmund made a rude sound. "Beauty is the devil's tool, meant to confound us."

Shaking his head at his clerk, Faucon gave the door another push, wanting to see the opposite side of the room. Where order reigned on the south side, chaos held sway to the north. What had surely started out as a normal household meal, with three tables all in a neat row and set with thick bread trenchers, horn cups and carved wooden spoons, was now a mess. Benches had been pushed this way and that as those sitting on them had leapt to join the hue and cry. Spoons lay scattered on the floor. One thick bread trencher had slid over the edge of a table, spilling whatever stew it had contained onto bench and floor. The far tabletop had been shoved almost off its braces, toppling horn cups of dark ale that was soaking into a once white tablecloth.

The door behind them opened. Faucon and Edmund turned as one. Little Jeanne exited, her eyes once more leaking tears. As she flew back down the steps, a slender young woman of no more than six-and-ten stepped unescorted onto the landing, her arms crossed before her. Despite her youth and grief, the girl bore herself with a certain confidence that told Faucon she was a daughter of this house.

That, and her attire. Her linen overgown was a pure deep blue, an expensive color, embroidered with a white diamond pattern. At the center of each diamond was a tiny star sewn from precious gold thread. Beneath her upper gown she wore a pale yellow undergown made of the finest wool.

She was no beauty, not with so long and narrow a face, but there was something inherently attractive about the arrangement of her features. Or there would have been, had her dark-brown eyes and nose not been swollen and reddened with grief. Her fair hair must have started the day contained in sober plaits. Now, one plait had lost its thong and had half-unraveled, while fine strands of hair straggled this way and that from the other braid.

Affording Edmund a mere glance, she gazed boldly at Faucon without according him the show of humility required of a woman when she confronted a man who was her equal or better. "I am Mistress Gisla. You are Sir Crowner?" she asked in Faucon's native French. Her pronunciation was flawless and her voice steadier and stronger than he expected.

Her introduction made him blink. Mistress? Did she claim that title because she was the master's daughter or because she was married to one of the man's sons? Perhaps she was the one that Peter the Webber was to have married.

"I am indeed, Mistress Gisla," Faucon replied with a brief nod of greeting. "I am Sir Faucon de Ramis, Crowner for this shire. It is now my duty, and not your sheriff's, to view your father's body and call the inquest jury. My apologies for intruding at such a time, but I must see him."

His request teased a ragged breath from her. As if she meant to hide her reaction from him, she looked away. That sent a strand of hair tumbling over her brow. In unconscious reaction, she lifted a hand to brush at it only to freeze as her gaze caught on her fingers.

They were foul with blood. So were the lower edges of the sleeves of both her gowns. Swallowing, she dropped her arm and closed her eyes for an instant. Tears dripped unheeded from her eyes.

"I have not even had time to summon the priest," she murmured, her voice so low that Faucon was certain she meant the words only for herself.

Then her resolve returned. Her eyes opened and she once more met his gaze without flinching. "Come with me," she said and started down the stairs.

With Edmund behind him, Faucon followed her to the ground floor. Mistress Gisla opened the small side door in the entryway, then stepped back, doing so without looking into the workshop beyond it. She drew a bracing breath. "Do as you must, sir, but I cannot escort you into this chamber."

"Nor need you enter," Faucon assured her. "There are three men of the guard outside, mistress. Send them to fetch your priest and to remind your menfolk who joined the hue and cry that they are now needed at home. When your servants have returned, send men to bear your father's body out of this chamber for you."

Edmund made a sound. "But the inquest jury," he began, his voice low.

"Cannot fit into this small chamber to do a proper viewing," Faucon finished, sending a chiding look at his clerk.

"Ah," Edmund breathed out in agreement.

Gisla looked from the clerk to the shire's new Crowner. Her gaze was flat, her eyes narrowed.

Without a word or an acknowledgment of what Faucon had said, she turned on her heel and rounded the larger open door to exit the house.

Signaling Edmund to stay where he stood, Faucon stepped into the workshop and ducked instinctively. Because it was located directly beneath the hall, this chamber had the same arrangement of columns and bays as the one above it. But here the arched ribs holding up the hall floor were much lower.

As he had noted from outside, the first two of the three small windows in the bays were closed, their solid wooden shutters held in place with wooden bars resting in metal brackets. The far window's bar lay on the floor beneath it. With its shutters thrown wide, enough light entered to show Faucon that the floor in here was slate, and that iron strapping bound each of the heavy wooden chests lining the walls and bays. All the chests were closed, each one secured with a keyed lock threaded through its metal straps.

A long high wooden worktable with a tall back stood against the wall opposite the windows. In one corner of the table was the checkered board that many merchants used for counting. Blood-drenched pennies were strewn across its surface. So too, had blood sprayed the worktable's tall back. Three thick wooden pegs studded that raised back panel. The one closest to the counting board held a handful of knotted measuring cords while two pairs of small scissors, neither of them longer than Faucon's hand, hung from the central peg.

The third peg, the one closest to the door was empty. Instead, the pair of scissors that must have hung from it now lay in two pieces on the floor in front of the table, beside the toppled stool on which Bernart le Linsman had been sitting before someone had slashed his throat.

Chapter Four

Dressed in a tunic made of the same blue fabric as his daughter's gown and a wool cloak lined with squirrel, Bernart lay on his left side. His left arm was crooked beneath him as if he might have had his hand pressed against his throat as he fell. A puddle of blood had formed on the floor beneath his throat. It had flowed away from him, following the level of the floor and filling the cracks and joints in the stonework as it grew.

Faucon crossed the chamber, stepping the way he would in the woodlands as he sought evidence of the prey he wished to follow. But here, what he hoped to find beneath his feet was the tale of Bernart's death.

Bloody smears marked the paths of those who had exited the chamber after the merchant's death. There were three clear sets. Two of these shoe prints were small. Mistress Gisla and Bernart's wife most likely, since the wife was said to have found her husband's body while his daughter had told him she'd been in the workshop prior to his arrival.

The third set was much larger and wider. All three sets of footprints pointed in only one direction, moving away from Bernart's body. Not surprising. Those who wore these shoes had only fouled their soles when they'd come to stand in the spreading blood near the fallen merchant.

Faucon dropped to one knee beside the corpse and pressed his fingers to Bernart's bare neck, beneath the edge of the man's neatly trimmed brown beard. The merchant yet retained the warmth of living. Then he touched the tip of his little finger to that pool of blood and frowned. It had already congealed into a thick gel, but that gel was beginning to separate. He'd seen that happen both on fields of battle as well as when hunting. Where blood pooled, it gelled, then after a time, it began to sweat out a clear liquid. While Bernart's warmth fit with the timing of the hue and cry and Peter the Webber's mad dash for sanctuary, which had occurred less than a quarter hour ago, that separation of the merchant's blood had Faucon thinking.

Turning Bernart's head upward, he studied the merchant's visage. It seemed that although the man hadn't recognized death coming for him when the one who killed him entered his workshop, he'd faced the end of his life with open eyes. The merchant wasn't a corpulent man, but there was something in Bernart's face that suggested he was one who ate deeply of life's riches, only to leave the table unsatisfied. The merchant and his daughter shared no common features save their deep brown eye color. Where Gisla was fair and her face narrow, her father's hair was brown and his face full. His features were small and soft, with a short nose and thick lips beneath his neatly-trimmed moustache.

The wound that had ended his life crossed his throat from ear to ear. Although it had started out fairly shallow, not completely parting the veins on the left side of his neck, it ended deep enough on his right side to guarantee Bernart a swift exit from life. The smooth edges of the gash suggested a well-honed blade, but then, a well-honed blade was what a man needed if he intended to open another man's throat.

Releasing the merchant's head, Faucon closed Bernart's eyes, wondering why neither mother nor daughter had thought to offer their kinsman that courtesy. Then, shifting on his knee, he eyed the two pieces of the scissors that lay on the floor. It was a tool of unusual design and size, with each blade almost the length of his forearm. The nearest half lay close by Bernart's feet and was coated with his blood.

Unable to believe that such a thing was weapon enough to do this deed, he picked up that bloody half. The blade was a well-made tool, to be sure. The metal had been worked until it felt almost as hard as his own sword. Faucon ran his thumb along its edge. Only toward the tip did it part the skin on his thumb. Although that surprised him, it didn't make the tool as sharp as he thought it should have been. Then again, a blade swiftly lost its edge when cutting through flesh and sinew.

He turned the half-scissors in his hand, once more examining the strange looking thing. All the shears he'd ever seen were made from one continuous piece of metal, bent into a loop to form a pair of intersecting knives. Indeed, that was how the two smaller pairs of scissors hanging on the worktable back were formed. Not so this pair. This one was two separate knives held together by some sort of a fastener inserted through the hole in the center of each blade.

He scanned the floor, seeking the fastener, a bolt of some sort no doubt. But with only one open window, it wasn't bright enough to find something as small as that bolt must be. Indeed, all he saw was the other half of the scissors.

Leaning to the side, he reached for the other half of the scissors only to freeze mid-gesture. As he moved, a shaft of dim light streamed over one shoulder to show him the floor beside his knee. There, outlined in spattered blood, was the shadow print of the front half of a shoe.

The huntsman in him came to vibrant life. Here was what he craved. This was spoor he could follow, a trail that would lead him to the murderer. Placing his hand into the outline, he spread and shaped his fingers as he sought to memorize its size and form.

"Might I use the stool, sir?" Edmund asked from the far end of the chamber where he yet stood.

Unwilling to risk his clerk disturbing what might be more of this shadowy spoor, Faucon rose and picked up the merchant's short stool. Holding it high, he handed the seat to Edmund, then turned to once more study the crisscrossing trails made by those exiting after Bernart's death. None of the prints matched the size and shape of the one outlined in blood, thus the owners of those shoes had done no wrong.

Stepping carefully, he opened the shutters on the closed windows, setting their bars on the top of the strongboxes. As this afternoon's bright light streamed in, it revealed a clean area on the floor near the shadow print. Of course. Bernart's body and the stool on which Edmund now sat had blocked the merchant's blood from reaching the floor here.

Faucon placed his right foot into the outlined print. His shoe completely covered it. Like Bernart, Faucon was a man of medium height, although he was more powerfully built than the merchant. The size of the print suggested that the one who had done this deed was a smaller man. Although that was certainly possible—small men could be as strong or stronger than some large men—for no reason Faucon could yet name, that felt improbable.

Leaving his right foot in the print, he shifted into the solid stance required of a killing stroke. That put his left foot at the center of the clean spot. Hence, the single outlined footprint.

Seeking to follow the same path as the murderer, Faucon reasoned out the line of events that resulted in Bernart's death. Entering the workshop, the killer had taken the scissors from the peg and disassembled it behind the merchant, doing so without stirring any concern from the man he meant to kill. Once the scissor blades were parted, the murderer had dealt his blow. But rather than jump back to avoid the spewing blood, he'd remained behind the merchant long enough to have his foot outlined on the floor.

Faucon frowned. When this particular injury was dealt well, as it had been here, there was no recourse for the victim save a swift death and an even swifter departure from consciousness. For blood to spew over the killer's shoe said that he'd held the merchant to the stool for a moment before releasing Bernart to the floor and his death throes. But why hold him at all?

Dissatisfied with what he conjured, Faucon stepped back, then looked down to see where his feet rested. He was in an area of the floor clean of blood spatter. Then again, most of what had spurted from Bernart's severed veins had shot to the sides, not reaching directly behind the man. There were no more outlined prints, and none of the existing bloody footprints matched the size of the killer's foot. Rather than blood-stained soles, this man would wear proof that he'd taken Bernart's life only on the top of his right shoe.

"I am ready, sir," Edmund said.

Faucon looked up. His clerk had set Bernart's stool just inside the workshop doorway. Once again, Edmund had his traveling desk in his lap, their all-important parchment spread across its slanted top. His quill, poised above the skin, glistened with fresh ink. He looked expectantly at his master.

"Bernart le Linsman has been murdered, his throat slashed," Faucon told him. "Although I cannot state exactly when he died, I do know that he's certainly been gone for longer than a half an hour. I say this because the blood that spilled from the linsman's neck is separating now that it has congealed."

Faucon once more tested the heft of the half scissors he held. As well-made as it was, the fact that it needed to be disassembled before it could be used as a weapon made it inconvenient. Why commit this deed with something so awkward when a well-honed knife might serve?

"Although I remain uncertain if this is an act of passion or one well-planned, the weapon used to kill Bernart was this half of the scissors." He showed Edmund what he held. "The man who plied it did so with his right hand, for the wound begins high on the left side of Bernart's throat and ends lower and far deeper on his right side. Whoever handled the blade was skilled in this sort of blow, for the cut is placed exactly where it should be to swiftly end a life."

Faucon grimaced as he said that. That information was hardly relevant. Anyone who'd ever slaughtered an animal knew how to use such a killing stroke, and that included just about everyone in this world.

"Also, the one who dealt the blow was strong enough to almost sever the linsman's windpipe. But the footprint he leaves behind suggests he was not a big man, I think," Faucon added, his voice trailing off into quiet. Again, the idea of the smaller man felt wrong.

"Good enough, sir," Edmund said and lowered his head as he set quill to parchment. "Bernart was murdered, his death caused by Peter the Webber, who slashed his throat with the scissors that he took from the worktable."

Faucon shot him sharp look. "That's not what I said."

"But it is all that the law requires," Edmund countered without looking up, his quill scratching out the words he, not his employer, wished to place on the parchment.

This was one battle Faucon would lose because Edmund was right. The law did not require him to describe more than the manner and classification of the death. But what satisfied the law left Faucon wanting much more.

"Well, do not yet ascribe this act to the webber," he commanded.

Edmund paused in his scribbling to look up. His brows lifted. "But this Peter was witnessed right here at the dead man's side. What of the hue and cry and the webber's plea for sanctuary? An innocent man doesn't run."

"He does if a mob is chasing him and he fears there will be no justice for him should he be caught," Faucon retorted, then sighed. "Edmund, remember that the miller was found beneath his wheel, but it was not the wheel that killed him. We wouldn't have known that had we not followed the trail left by the man who had truly done murder."

Edmund studied his master for a moment. "Aye, and the man who committed that crime yet evades the earthly justice that is his due. I hope he doesn't believe he'll so easily escape heavenly justice when his time comes." The clerk's eyes took light. "Do you think he has done the same here?"

Faucon smiled. Edmund was far too literal. "Nay, not him. Never again him, and so he well knows." The time for that one's accusation and arrest had come and gone, but so had the man's freedom to do as he pleased in this shire.

"My point is only to ask you to humor me," he told his clerk. "Just as it's not in you to ignore the law, I cannot blindly accept what others tell me is true, or even what appears to be true, without verifying it for myself. Let me hunt for the one who did this in my own way."

Edmund watched him for another moment, then offered a single nod. "As you will, sir. I can leave space on the parchment to record the webber's name later, when you have proved it to yourself."

Then, rising from the stool, the clerk set his lap desk on the same chest where he had carefully arranged his stone, his inkpot and his knife. After exactly positioning his quill across the top of the desk, he turned to look at his master.

"Now that we are satisfied the linsman was indeed murdered, it is time to confirm that he was born an Englishman and not a Norman," the monk said evenly. "Since neither the wife nor daughter may swear to this, and there appears to be no other man of consequence in the house at the moment, I would like to call his neighbors to testify. Indeed, as they attest to Master Bernart's ancestry, perhaps they will also agree to stand surety for the wife, guaranteeing that she makes her appearance before the court when called to swear that she was the first finder."

Having expected more of an argument from Edmund, Faucon watched his clerk in surprise. "As you should," he agreed.

"I'll come for you when I have returned here with the neighbors, sir," Edmund said, then crossed his arms, tucking his hands into his sleeves, and sighed. "What a shame that they cannot offer vows in place of the wife, swearing for her that she was the first finder."

"Why would they need to?" Faucon countered. "A woman can be named as first finder, and be called to court to testify to the same."

"Of course she can. I just don't wish to deal with her," Edmund retorted.

He shuddered. The movement was a mummer's portrayal of disgust. "All the tears. It's so unseemly." Pivoting, he left the workshop.

Chapter Five

Faucon grinned at that. "I'll take the woman's vow without you then," he called after his clerk.

Indeed he would, and happily so. Not only did it give him the excuse he needed to intrude on the new widow's grief with his questions, it also gave him the chance to ask what he would without worrying over what Edmund might blurt out.

"As you should, you being our Coronarius, sir," the monk called back from outside the house. It was the first time Faucon had heard the clerk admit such a thing.

Grateful to have this unexpected moment alone with his thoughts, Faucon once more scanned the linsman's workshop. This time his gaze came to rest on the checkered counting board and its stacks of pennies. There was no interruption in the spattering of Bernart's blood across the coins. So, what the merchant had laid out on the board before his death remained where he'd placed it after his passing. That said thievery wasn't the reason for the man's death.

The coins on the right side of the board were jumbled across its surface, some having even spilled over the back edge. Those on the board's left side remained neatly stacked, some in piles as high as six pence. Faucon closed his eyes, imagining Bernart in the instant before the blade had been pulled across his throat.

The man standing behind the merchant would have grabbed his victim's head with his left hand as he began to ply his weapon. That was why the coins on the left of the board were undisturbed. In Bernart's surprise at being grabbed by one he trusted, he'd instinctively tried to catch his attacker's hand with his own. His left arm had come straight up from the table, not touching any of the coins, but his right had briefly swept across the board before he lifted his arm. Thus, the tumbled coins closest to that edge.

Again, Faucon crouched near Bernart to reexamine the slash across his throat. This time, he looked at its depth at the left side of the man's neck. Even if Bernart had managed to stop the killer's hand, preventing the stroke from being finished, it had been too late. Aye, this cut had grown bolder as it progressed, but enough damage had been done with the first bite of that strange blade to guarantee the merchant's life would throb out of him in tune with the beat of his heart.

Coming to his feet, he once more studied the counting board, again eyeing the coins and their arrangement, unable to shake his sense of dissatisfaction. The varying number in each column had the look of a master calculating the wages he owed his workers, or perhaps the sums he owed his suppliers for what they'd delivered. He caught his breath. Coins weren't the only item needed when making such payments! Where were the tally sticks on which a man of business noted whom he'd paid and how much? And where had the coins he'd been counting out come from?

The worktable was too dark and the light in here too dim to show him where blood had landed on the bench. He ran his fingertips from the edge of the counting board to where he was certain the blood spurting from Bernart's severed veins couldn't reach. Aye, there were places where he felt dried blood, but there wasn't enough to leave the sort of tale he'd found on the floor.

Turning, he eyed the chests lining the walls. None were unlocked, much less open. What sort of man kept his treasure chest locked in the middle of a task that might require him to return to it for yet more coins? Certainly not the sort of man who trusted as completely as Bernart. Nay, such a man as he would have thrown wide that chest, and left it so while he worked.

Was that why the murderer had lingered after dealing Bernart the killing blow? To return Bernart's counting tools to an open chest that he then closed and locked? Aye, to safely store the tally sticks but not the coins. That mad thought brought Faucon 'round full circle to ponder the timing of Peter's flight to the church and sanctuary.

No more than half an hour had passed since the webber had made his run. But Bernart had been dead for at least three times as long, if not longer. Putting away the tally sticks couldn't have taken but a moment or two. If Peter had done this, why had he lingered here any longer after he'd closed that lock? He had to have known that every moment he stayed, his chance of being discovered increased.

Faucon breathed out in new frustration. Of a sudden, the conversation he craved was with the webber. Aye, and he was just as certain that he wasn't ready to speak with Mistress Alina. But taking the first finder's vow might be his only opportunity to have a private conversation with her. As for the Peter the Webber, Faucon suspected heaven would have to move before the elderly priest allowed him inside his realm to speak to the man.

That left him once more studying that shadowy spoor. The tale it told was clear. Bernart had never imagined that it was Death coming for him, not when the killer entered his workroom nor when the man disassembled the scissors next to him, not even when this one stepped up close behind. Not only had Bernart known the one who'd finished him, the linsman had trusted this man with his very life.

What was unfortunate for Bernart was a boon for Faucon since tracking such a man should be easy enough. All he need do was discover who the linsman might have loved that much, then look at that man's shoes. Surely that would be easy enough to accomplish. It was hard to imagine taking forty days to sniggle out who had wielded this strange blade and ended Bernart's life.

"My pardon, sir," said a man from the workshop doorway, "but the mistress has asked us to bring our master into the hall."

Faucon turned. Two burly men, both barely more than youths, stood in the opening. They looked to be kin, having the same wide faces, brown eyes and hair. Like the women of the household, they wore pale blue linen tunics, in this case over yellow chausses. Although both men offered him the bows expected of servants as they greeted their betters, one man did so without lifting his attention from his shoes.

"Aye, you may remove your master," Faucon told the man who met his gaze, "but I think the hall is not the place to take him. I'll be calling the inquest jury soon. I cannot imagine your mistress wants all the men of this town tramping through her house."

This one offered him a twisted smile. "It was said you are new to our vale, sir. Here in Stanrudde, we pay our king for the right to call inquest juries only from the parish where the act took place. Men of commerce do not much care for the interruption such a jury and its duties makes in their day, especially when the victim comes from an area of town they know little about.

"As for where we take Master Bernart," he continued, "what Mistress Gisla commands, we must do. She is her father's heir and now our employer."

"What?!" Faucon blurted out in astonishment. "There are no sons? You are not his journeymen?"

"Nay, not we," the speaker said with a shake of his

head. "We are but day laborers here. God rest them, the master's sons never lived long enough to learn any trade. As for journeymen, the master needed no apprentice save for Mistress Gisla. The needlework and trade that is practiced within these walls doesn't belong to Master Bernart, but to his wife. Thus, just as Mistress Alina taught Mistress Gisla to use her needle, our master schooled his daughter in his only trade, that being selling what the women of this household make." Here, he shrugged. "That, and managing those of us who work for his house."

"This trade belongs to a woman?" Faucon gaped at that.

The man nodded, the look on his face saying this wasn't the first time he'd explained the facts of his household to another of his sex. "Aye, so it does and so it shall remain, passing to Mistress Gisla after Mistress Alina's death, if she so wills. As for my brother and me, as well as most of the other men who labor in this house," the sweep of the servant's hand was meant to include those absent men, "we earn our bread by cutting and wrapping fabric."

Faucon's thoughts reeled as everything he held true about the world turned on its head. A woman as master of her own trade while her husband was no more than a costermonger, hawking what she made? Other than alewives, whose trade didn't befit a man, who had heard of such a thing? Then again, perhaps it could be said that the needlework these women did here also didn't befit a man. Although judging by this house and its fixtures, perhaps it should.

As he digested all that the man had said, Faucon caught his breath. Gisla was Bernart's sole heir. That meant she must also be Peter's betrothed.

Why in God's name would the webber have murdered his future father-by-marriage when all this wealth would be his once he wed Gisla, something that couldn't be too far in the future, given the girl's age? Even if what the servant said was true—that the riches here would never actually belong to Peter—it would still be his to enjoy, just as Bernart had enjoyed the fruits of his wife's work.

Of a sudden, the quiet man made a strangled noise. He leapt into the chamber and snatched up the half scissors that yet lay on the floor. Holding it up, he showed it to his companion. "My scissors! The bolt is missing and they are undone. Tom, how am I to cut my pieces if I don't have it to use?"

"That can't be yours, Rob," Tom told him. "You left your scissors in the storehouse when we went to take our meat."

"But of course they're mine," Rob returned. "There is no other tool like them in the house, and so you well know. Brother, help me! I must find the bolt, and where is the other half?" he cried out in rising panic as he once more scanned the floor.

"I have the other blade," Faucon replied, moving his hand a little to indicate he held the half but not lifting it far enough to reveal it to the men.

As he spoke, he eyed their shoes. The brothers wore the usual working man's soft leather boots, with uppers that rose above their ankles and were tied in place. Their footwear was well-worn and stained, but only with the manure and muck found in a city lane. Moreover, both men's feet were longer and wider than the mark on the floor.

"What of the bolt? Have you found the bolt?" Rob was almost sobbing.

"I have not," Faucon replied, with a shake of his head.

"God save me," Rob murmured and dropped to his knees and began patting the floor around the spot where the second blade had lain.

Faucon watched Rob in some surprise. It was the

rare workman who didn't have what he needed to repair what he used on a day-to-day basis. "Surely, you have other bolts for your tool."

"We don't!" Rob cried. "These scissors are beyond expensive. The master said there is no other like them in all of this shire or mayhap all this land. He bought them from some foreign merchant when he was in London last, three months ago. All I know is that the metal is harder than my own knife and they hold an edge like no other shears I've used."

"As special as that?" Faucon asked.

"Aye, it is," Tom said, dropping to his knees to aid his brother in searching for the bolt. "The master bought it because Rob needs scissors that cut cleanly. His job is to shape the finest linen Roger the Webber can produce into the proper forms for making the headdresses and wimples that the well-born ladies love. It's Rob's to do because his hand is the steadiest of us all. If his scissors aren't sharp enough, the fabric puckers and threads pull as he cuts. That mars the finished piece, reducing its value. So aye, Rob sharpens often and straightens even more often than he sharpens. That's because the master reclaims the cost of Rob's errors from his wages," Tom added, a hint of resentment in his voice.

Faucon's brows rose. That Tom would say as much out loud to a stranger suggested that unlike the men of the hue and cry, Bernart was not so well-loved in his own household, at least not by his manservants.

He extended his hand, offering Tom the half scissors he held. "Perhaps it would be better to search for the bolt once your master's body has been removed," he suggested.

"Holy Mother!" Tom cried out as he saw the bloody blade. Rob looked up from the floor. His face went ashen and he crossed himself.

"Aye, I fear you'll have some cleaning to do," Faucon

said. "This was used to cut your master's throat and end his life. Tell me, for I need to know. How did the man who took your scissors from you do it without you noticing, especially since they are as precious as you say?"

Rob sat back his heels. His hand trembled as he took the blade from Faucon, then he turned his gaze to the floor. "I care for my master's tools. I would never allow anyone to take so precious an implement from me, certainly not without the master's permission. My scissors weren't missing when I left the storehouse for our meal. I placed them on my worktable as I always do, on top of the fabric I was cutting. The scissors are heavy and so you now know, sir, since you've held that blade. That's weight enough to restrain the fine linen I cut. Otherwise, the fabric is so thin that even the smallest breath of air can send it drifting."

Faucon remembered seeing the breeze lift the length of cloth off a table when he entered the linsman's courtyard. Then he frowned, catching the full meaning of Rob's comment. "You were at your meat but your master was not at the table with you?" he asked.

Such a thing was almost unheard of. The man who purchased the food always presided over the meal he gave as a gift to his household. But then, in this household it was the woman who made that gift.

Rob shrugged but Tom replied. "Such a thing is not unusual for the master these days," he said uneasily, his gaze shifting to the side.

"Your master never eats with those who serve him?" Faucon persisted.

Again, Tom shifted uneasily. "Nay, he always joins us, it's just that he's always late. It happened only occasionally until he returned from that London trip. Since then, it's happened so often that we no longer wait for him to join us before beginning our meal. If we did, we'd never be able to finish our afternoon tasks."

Faucon looked askance at that. There was something strange afoot in this household, something strange indeed.

Tom continued. "Only when Mistress Alina can no longer tolerate the master's absence does she go to fetch him." His words faded into silence as he looked at his brother. "Rob," he whispered, "he came into the storehouse and took your scissors so he could do this terrible deed."

"God help me," Rob pleaded, his request for heavenly intervention a bare breath. He came to his feet, backing carefully into the doorway before he briefly raised his gaze to meet Faucon's.

"Master Peter must have taken my scissors when he came creeping in through our gate like a thief in the night, intent on wrongdoing. Fie on me! Hadn't I just honed the edge to its sharpest? The mistress had told me there would be a special piece for me to cut right after the meal ended, and I should be ready to get to it the moment I returned to work."

"And this request, was it unusual for your mistress to make?" Faucon wanted to know.

That made Rob frown in surprise. "Nay, not so much," he answered hesitantly. "She's always doing odd pieces."

Tom came to his feet and joined his brother in the doorway. "It's become our mistress's habit to ask Rob for these cuts ever since the master bought these scissors. As I said, these scissors make a wondrous cut, so much cleaner than any other."

Well, that was one question satisfied. It had been planning and not passion at the root of Bernart's death. But whose planning?

"Why would Peter the Webber wish to murder your master?" he asked of the two.

They stared back at him, their expressions identical, both empty and confused. And, a little frightened that a knight might be asking them such a question.

Faucon smiled. "Pay me no mind," he said. "Instead, do your master one final service as you bear him to where the inquest jury will view him. Know that I'll suggest to your mistress that place should be the courtyard, but wait to take him until she confirms this with you. While you wait, search for your bolt as you will. Let me know if you find it."

Chapter Six

Leaving Bernart in the care of his servants, Faucon made his way back up the stairs to the hall door. It now stood open wide. Inside, Gisla, her hair once more neatly plaited, and three men, dressed in tunics the same color as those worn by Rob and Tom, were clearing away the remains of the aborted meal. While the servants removed the implements and platters, Gisla was putting sodden bread trenchers into a large alms basket for distribution to Stanrudde's poor.

Mistress Alina's apprentices and journeywomen had also returned to the chamber, but their activities were far less useful and definitely not profitable. Yet trapped in their distress, they had gathered into the sunlit bays, not to ply their needles but to clutch together, murmuring and sighing like unhappy doves.

Faucon stepped inside the room, catching Gisla's eye. She set her basket on a bench and joined him. He wasn't surprised to see she had scoured her hands, doing so until her fingers were reddened. Once again, she offered him no sign of respect as she stood before him. Perhaps her rudeness was the result of being raised in a household that was turned on its head. Placing women above men was like declaring Man had the right to sit in judgment of God.

"You have requested your father's body be brought into the hall," Faucon said, burying his disapproval of her and her household behind a quick smile. "However, I'll be calling the inquest jury to confirm the verdict of murder, doing so before nightfall. I think it might

68

better serve you to place your sire in your courtyard where all can see him without intruding upon your mourning. Once your neighbors have rendered their verdict and viewed him, you may care for him as you will."

There was the slightest softening in her expression. "Ah, you said as much before. I wasn't thinking," she added. "Aye, I'll see he's taken to the courtyard for you. My thanks." Her words were flat and lacking in all gratitude.

Even knowing what this might cost him, Faucon couldn't resist testing her. "By the bye, I struggle to convince myself that Peter the Webber killed your sire."

Her eyes flew wide. Her face whitened and she began to crumple. Startled, he grabbed her by the upper arms to steady her. Her head bowed, her breath coming in tiny gasps, she wrapped her hands around his forearms, holding herself upright. When she had regained her composure and steadied on her feet, she opened her hands to push back from him, her head yet bowed.

"Mary, please save him," she whispered.

Then, she fled past Faucon and down the stairs, shooting him only the swiftest of glances as she went. It was all he needed to see of her face to know that Gisla la Linswoman loved her betrothed with all her heart.

Startled and pleased that he had generated that bit of information with so little effort, he added it to all the other bits he'd collected thus far. The need to speak with Peter the Webber once again niggled at him. Forty days was too long to wait. The sooner the webber told his tale, the sooner Faucon could drive his true prey out into the open and have him arrested.

He shifted to look at the women gathered to the south side of the chamber. To a one they now watched him in an interest far bolder than was appropriate for their sex. He nodded to them.

"Your mistress was the first finder. As required by the law, I must take her oath, doing so in our king's name. Who among you will lead me to her and stay at her side to comfort her as I say what I must?"

"I will, Sir Crowner."

One of the older women came to her feet. As tall as he, her plaited hair was fair and her head uncovered, suggesting that she remained unmarried. Time had been kind to her, despite that she was in her middle years, adding only faint lines at the corners of her eyes and either side of her mouth. That left her yet a pretty woman with a round face, blue eyes and the lush lips that men found attractive.

The needlewoman shook out her skirts as if to brush off the day's upset, then looked at the others in the bay with her. "Aye, we've all done enough mourning and moaning for the now," she told them. "On the morrow we'll be called to honor our master at his wake. It will reflect poorly on our house and us if we open our hall when it's at less than its best. Up Ella, Tilda and Jeanne. Run to the warehouse and fetch the covering cloths for the frames."

"Aye, mistress," said all three of the youngest girls as one, leaping to their feet.

Their use of the title 'mistress' piqued Faucon's interest for it pronounced the older woman accomplished at her trade. But if that were so, why did she still live with her master, or her mistress as was the case here? In every occupation, including his own, there was a time for learning and a time for leaving. A squire became a knight after he'd mastered the skills of dealing out death, whether man-to-man or on the battle-field. Once a squire received his coleé and his title, he departed from his foster father's home to make his own way in the world. Then again, perhaps a woman's trade was different than those practiced by men.

As the three young girls trotted past him and down the stairs, this mistress spoke to the other women. "Bestir yourselves, all of you. First, see to it that our work is folded away and properly protected, and the frames moved into the corners where they cannot be disturbed or marked by unthinking hands or curious fingers. After that, we'll all of us be in the kitchen, else there won't be anything decent to feed those who come to pay their respects upon the morrow."

That elicited groans from a few of those she commanded, but they all did as she bid. As these women began gathering up their work, the needlewoman crossed the hall to join Faucon. She offered him the show of respect that the daughter of this house had not.

"I am Mistress Nanette, Sir Crowner." She pointed toward the door across the landing. "Mistress Alina is in her chamber. If you will?"

Faucon exited the hall ahead of her, only to stop when they were both on the landing, hoping she would allow him a private moment. "I must tell you, Mistress Nanette. This house and its trade are like none I've ever seen."

That made her smile, the movement of her mouth filling her face and blue eyes with lively amusement. "I can imagine our work must seem strange indeed, especially to a newcomer. I expect I'd say the same were I to see this house and what we do for the first time. But I long ago forgot my amazement over how the Lord saw fit to turn us all upon our ears, and now only remember how much it was to my benefit."

Faucon cocked his head at that, the motion encouraging her to continue. She did.

"I came into this house as barely more than a babe, the extra daughter of a poor man sold to the master as a kitchen lass. And that's what I did—swept ashes from the oven and hearth—for several years. Of course, that was back when the apprentices in this house were still all lads learning how to make flax into linen, then how to turn that fabric into the braies and head scarves that one expects from a lindraper."

"What changed?" Faucon asked when it seemed that Nanette might go no further with her tale.

His question made Mistress Nanette's eyes sparkle. "Mistress Elinor, the old master's wife," she replied. "She was a woman who couldn't bear waste. She took the scraps left from her husband's projects and turned them into ribbons decorated by her hand with colorful threads. It was a skill she'd learned from some relative, and one that gave her joy. This she did only to please herself but the old master didn't complain. Although the time she stole for her bits and pieces might have been used for his business, her work always sold, even if it didn't generate much additional profit for the house.

"Then one day her designs caught the eye of our abbot, the one who ruled before this new one." The movement of her hand and sharp lift of her brows as she spoke suggested she thought little of Abbot Athelard. "He begged the mistress to make him a few yards in a specific pattern. It was a gift, he told her, but didn't mention for whom his gift was intended. Shortly after she had delivered what he requested, a royal messenger arrived. Our old queen–our present king's mother–sent words of praise for Mistress Elinor's work and asked for more ribbons, yards and yards more, in that same particular pattern. The price offered for the work was, indeed, princely."

Faucon's brows rose at that. Nanette laughed at his surprised look. "Exactly our reaction, sir. You cannot imagine the panic created by such a request! In an instant, the master gave up head scarves and undergarments, making room instead for the mistress's new frames. Every nimble finger in the household, mine included, even though as a servant I had neither the right nor the coin to tread where apprentices did, was put to work satisfying our queen."

Her smile widened into a pleased grin at the memory. "That day, I went from a life of drudgery to one that filled my heart with joy, doing so at no cost to me or my family. As you can see from our present house, Mistress Elinor did better than please her new customer. More requests followed, and, as others of the royal court saw our work, they weren't just from our queen. Before long, our old master owned the fields in which the flax was grown, the looms in which the threads were woven, and the pots in which the finished fabric and our threads were bleached so Stanrudde's dyers could give them the most fashionable hues.

"Thus did the growing and processing of flax into linen, and the preparation of linen fabric for our handiwork become the trades that the old master taught to those of his apprentices who stayed after the change. All his journeymen left to find new masters, not caring for, or perhaps not seeing the advantage for themselves in our strange new trade. Meanwhile, Mistress Elinor began training her own apprentices, including me. She liked my use of colors," Nanette added, her gaze softening and filling with fondness for her former mistress.

"The others call you 'mistress,' but if that is your proper title, why do you yet remain in the house?" Faucon asked, more from curiosity than any need to probe. Just as he had been granted the right to call himself 'knight' instead of 'squire' after his ceremony, journeymen couldn't be called 'master' until they'd been judged competent in their skills by their peers.

Nanette looked at him as if his question surprised her. "They name me so because I have earned that title. I completed my masterwork, one that fetched me a pretty penny, too."

"Then, why haven't you left to form your own house?" he persisted in confusion.

That made her laugh again. It was the sound of a woman well-pleased with her life. "Form my own house? Where would I put such a house? Nor do I have an interest in any other sort of commerce. Nay, there are only a very few who can afford to buy what I and the other women in this house have learned to make. I know well what my talents are and they don't include dealing with the sort of fine folk who buy our wares. That was the skill the old master discovered and nurtured in Master Bernart, and why the master married him to Mistress Alina. Master Bernart knows..." she paused to sigh, her eyes suddenly glistening.

If the manservants of the house resented their master, it seemed that wasn't the case for the women here. She cleared her throat and began again.

"The master always knew just what to say to please bishop and baron alike. It's a skill that he passed on to his daughter. Although," she paused, then sighed again.

"Although?" Faucon asked, daring to pry where he had no right. But her tale stirred more questions than it answered.

"Although Mistress Gisla is a woman," Nanette finished with a shrug. "I wonder how well the high and mighty will like trading coins with her instead of the master they expect. Despite what skills we might have in our trade, men expect to deal with other men when they make a purchase, especially one as costly as those made here. What a pity none of the master's sons survived."

"Such is the world in which we live," Faucon said.

She nodded at that. "And that is why I'm content to serve out my days here, saving what I earn for that time when my fingers are no longer nimble enough to ply my needle. Meanwhile, I happily train Mistress Alina's apprentices so that they can do what I have—support their families as they claim a life far easier than they ever expected to own."

Then, restoring the cobwebs to her memories, she started past Faucon toward the door on the opposite side of the landing. Her expression remained amused, as if she yet laughed inwardly at the idea of owning her own trade. "Come with me, sir," she said, already starting through the opening, "and ask your questions of our mistress."

The chamber beyond the door was the mirror image of the hall, lined with columns and bays, each bay set with a tall window, but the shutters were closed, leaving the room cloaked in shadows. Enough light streamed in through the open door behind him to reveal that each bay was filled with neatly stacked pallets and folded blankets. If this house was similar to the others Faucon knew, then this was where the female apprentices and journeywomen, as well as any female servants, slept. As a rule, all a household's womenfolk, no matter their age or rank, slept close to the protection of their master and out of the reach of the household's male members, who generally made their beds in cellars, kitchens or workshops.

A short wooden wall separated the final bay at the back of the chamber from the rest of the room. Although the wall didn't reach the ceiling, it was enough of a barrier to create a private space. The door at its center stood ajar. Nanette tapped lightly but didn't wait for an answer before she pushed open the panel and stepped inside.

The room within was trapped in a gloomy dimness, what with the wall blocking the light from the landing and the shutters closed. Despite that, there could be no missing the bed that filled almost the whole space. Only a queen's love for pretty gowns could have generated income enough to purchase such a piece. It was massive—as wide as two men and nearly as long. Four posts the size of small trees held aloft a wooden ceiling.

He dared to step closer and touch the nearest post. His fingers found it had been carved in the same style as the columns on the wall. The curtains that hung from the wooden ceiling were pulled shut around the bed, enclosing the inhabitant.

Nanette crossed to the north-facing window and pushed back one shutter panel. As muted light tumbled in to drive off the dimness, the top half of the merchant's green brocaded bed curtains took fire, glittering like gold. Faucon caught his breath. It glittered like gold because that was what it was—cloth of gold, fabric woven from threads of gold.

Last month he might have eaten his heart out over such a piece and choked after on sour envy. But then, a month ago he had been a second son with no prospects for improving his life save to pray that the Lord might take his mother and elder brother before their time, something he could never do.

No longer. Upon Faucon's elevation to Crowner, he'd become the master of a fine stone house in Blacklea Village that came with its own bed. To be sure it wasn't as fine as this one, but it was his and his alone.

"Who is it?" a woman asked from inside the enclosing curtains, her voice a rasping croak.

"'Tis me, mistress," Nanette said. "I bring with me the king's knight. Sir Crowner he's called. He must speak with you regarding the master's death."

There was a rustling, suggesting that the mattress inside that fine frame was only stuffed with straw. "A knight? Does he come from our sheriff?"

"Nay mistress, I do not," Faucon replied on his own behalf. Although he raised his voice so she could hear him, he kept his tone gentle as befitted addressing one so newly aggrieved. "Our archbishop has removed the responsibility for viewing the dead and calling the inquest juries, from England's sheriffs and given them instead to certain knights in each shire. I am Sir Faucon de Ramis, now of Blacklea Village, and the knight who has assumed these duties for this shire. My pardon for disturbing you at such a time, but you are the first finder. The law requires that I receive from you a vow to appear at court when the justices call for you."

A long moment of silence followed his words. Just when he'd begun to wonder if Mistress Alina intended to reply, the wooden curtain rings on the far side of the bed scraped quietly over their pole. "Nanette," the woman within cried softly, "come to me."

Nanette shot Faucon a swift sidelong look, then disappeared around the corner of the bed. Low-voiced hissing ensued. Although Faucon could make out only a word or two of the conversation they shared, he had no trouble recognizing Mistress Alina's anger at his intrusion. Nor could he doubt Nanette's place in the household. The woman who had expected to do no more than sweep ashes from a hearth boldly countered her mistress's irritation with soothing words.

There was silence for a moment, then Nanette returned around the corner of the bed. "You may come, sir," she said, no sign in her expression that anything untoward had occurred.

Faucon followed her to stop a decent distance from where Mistress Alina sat, bathed in the muted glow from the unshuttered window. Her feet were bare and she wore a set of pale orange gowns lacking the elaborate decoration that covered her daughter's attire. She was unnaturally pale, something that Faucon credited to grief and shock.

The new widow was swiftly braiding her uncovered honey-colored hair. Like her daughter, her features were long and narrow, but Mistress Alina's face was more square, her chin and jaw strong, and her

cheekbones more defined. Although Faucon guessed
that Alina and Nanette were of an age, both of them
being no more than ten years his senior, time had laid
its map more heavily on Alina, webbing her skin. Deep
crevices marked the corners of her eyes and either side
of her mouth.

Although he needed no further confirmation that
this was Gisla's mother beyond Alina's visage, if he'd
wanted it, he could have found it in her manner. Like
her daughter, she had none of a woman's proper
humility. As Nanette sat beside her mistress on the
bed, taking over the task of plaiting, Faucon offered the
new widow a deep bow.

"Mistress," he said by way of introduction.

Mistress Alina watched him hollow-eyed. "What is
this vow you need from me?"

"You must swear that you'll appear before the
justices when they arrive in Stanrudde to examine the
matter of your husband's murder," Faucon replied.
"They'll want to hear from your own lips that you were
the first to find Master Bernart after his death, and that
you then rightfully raised the hue and cry, urging your
neighbors to seek out his murderer."

He paused to watch her closely. "This you can do
because both of these things are true, aye?"

Nanette spoke for her mistress. "Aye, they are. She
was the first finder."

Faucon ignored the woman, keeping his gaze on
Bernart's widow. "These things are true?" he repeated.
"You were the first finder?"

"I was," Mistress Alina replied, her voice as hollow
as her eyes. "Nanette says I must also leave my bed to
seek out my neighbors, asking them to guarantee that
I will come to court when called."

"Ah," Faucon said, understanding a little better her
reluctance to speak with him. It startled him that
Nanette might have said as much to her.

Because the process of justice in these far-flung shires was so slow—it sometimes took many years before the justices in eyre circled around to a distant locale—first finders, as well as witnesses, often lost their enthusiasm for participating in a trial that had seemed so urgent years earlier. Sometimes even the attestors, those who had begged for justice in the first place, refused to appear when called, having settled or forgotten the original matter over the years. But every complaint that wasn't heard cost England's king a penny or two, the fee that was charged for each complaint brought before the justices. To stem this steady trickle of forfeited silver, the law required four of the first finder's neighbors to swear on pain of incurring their own fine to deliver the finder to court.

"Nay, there's no need for you to leave your chamber. My clerk is presently seeking out your neighbors so they can promise on your behalf," he assured her, then hesitated. Once he had her oath, she could rightfully dismiss him and he would have to comply, when he craved more from her.

"What I need to hear from you at this moment is your oath to appear at court when called and also a description of how and when you found Master Bernart," he said, taking Edmund's precious law and twisting it a little.

"Must she swear upon anything?" Nanette asked as Mistress Alina yet hesitated.

"Nay," Faucon shook his head. "Mistress Alina's word will suffice."

The widow sighed at that, her shoulders relaxing. "I vow to appear when called upon to do so by the justices. When I stand before them, I will testify that I saw Peter the Webber kill my husband. After that, I raised the hue and cry as I knew I should," she said, her voice rasping again.

Then she buried her face into her hands. "May God

take Peter! How could he have done this?" she cried into her palms.

"Hush, sweetling," Nanette murmured, wrapping her arm around her mistress and rocking the woman a little.

Alina pushed her away. "Nay, I cannot hush!" she cried out.

Her grief propelled her to her feet, proving that she was as tall as Faucon. Like some women, her form was thin as one of her needles above her waist, while heavier around her hips and her womb. She paced past the stranger in her bedchamber to its door where she threw her arms wide.

"That arrogant fool! Bernart did this to himself. Did he think that Gisla wouldn't tell Peter?"

Faucon watched her, content to wait. The merchant's wife did not disappoint. Whirling, she started back toward him.

"Or that Peter wouldn't be outraged over the news?" she nearly shouted as she passed him, then again dropped to sit on the bed.

"So your daughter's betrothed had good reason to wish your husband dead," he said. It was a comment, not a question.

Alina lifted her gaze to meet his. Faucon raised his brows. As much as Gisla loved her betrothed, Mistress Alina hated her husband. It was written for all the world to read in her expression.

"My daughter isn't betrothed to Peter the Webber or any other man," she told him.

"'Struth?" Faucon asked in surprise. "I joined the hue and cry as we chased the webber," he told her. "When the man Hodge confronted Father Herebert, trying to breach Peter's claim to sanctuary, he named the webber your daughter's betrothed."

"So would any man in Stanrudde do," Nanette replied, nodding.

"And that man would be just as mistaken as Hodge," Alina retorted. "Nay, when Bernart and I last spoke of Gisla's marriage not but a month or so ago, his intention was to wed her to some Londoner. Oh, there was a time when my husband considered a union between our house and Roger's, wishing to reunite two pieces of the trade my father tore apart so that each of the journeymen he loved would have a business of their own."

She glanced up at Faucon. "Bernart and Roger, and Hodge as well, were my father's apprentices when my mother's trade supplanted my father's. They won my father's affection by their loyalty, by remaining with him and our house after all the others left," she added in bitter explanation.

Then her mouth twisted. "But the plan to wed Gisla and Peter occurred five years ago, when Bernart and Roger yet shared some fondness for each other. Now, all their affection is gone, killed by Bernart. He discarded his friend, just as he wished to discard me and my love for him." The rancor in her voice alone suggested that her husband's dislike for her wasn't the first time she'd experienced his betrayal.

"Oh aye, Bernart continued to make sly suggestions about the union of our children to Roger, but they were only the pretenses of promises. No vows of betrothal have ever been spoken between Gisla and Peter, nor is there a written contract describing the terms of their union."

She freed a harsh breath. "That was Bernart. Full of clever words and pretty phrases, talking, always talking, until you believed he'd agreed with you and would provide what you requested. Then, when you finally demanded he produce what you thought he'd promised, his vows would prove empty."

Punctuating her remark with a brusque shrug, she stared at her chamber door, her gaze boring holes through the thick wood. "Woe to anyone beneath the rank of baron if they believed a word he said to them."

Faucon nodded. He'd known a few with this sort of character. Generally, they'd been men of much charm and wit, but, because they lacked all honor, their word could never be trusted. The proof that Bernart was of their ilk was in the manner of his death. Departing life on the edge of a blade was a common fate for those who broke their word too often.

That made him reconsider the affection shown by the hue and cry. If Bernart had been this sort of man, it was hardly likely he'd be that beloved by his community. Or that so many men would be set on delivering instant justice to his murderer. Who then did they love, if not Bernart?

"How was it that you happened to be in the workshop at the instant of your husband's death?" he asked.

"I had come down from the hall to call my husband to the table for our meal," she replied, supplying the answer he expected.

"And when you stepped into the workroom you saw Peter the Webber. What was he doing when you entered?" he asked carefully, hoping to guide her where he needed her to go.

"Aye, I saw him," Alina shot back, her words as sharp as the scissors used on Bernart. She looked directly at him, her dark gaze no less well-honed. "He was kneeling at Bernart's side as my husband lay on the floor, bleeding his last. The bloody blade was still in his hand."

It took all Faucon's will not to react as she described seeing the impossible. "What did you do when you saw this and realized what Peter had done?"

That made the widow frown. She glanced at Nanette. The other woman reached out a hand in invitation. Alina twined her fingers with Nanette's, then shifted on the bed to better study Faucon.

"What did I do?" she repeated in confusion. "What else, save what I just vowed to tell the justices when they come? I screamed that he had done murder to Bernart. I called for my household to take him."

"So she did," Nanette agreed. "We all heard her from the table."

"But even before I raised my voice, Peter had seen me and was racing past me for the door," Alina said, speaking over the other woman. "I followed him into the courtyard, still screaming of murder and calling for my servants and neighbors to stop him."

"As you should have done," Faucon assured her, smiling a little. "And then you returned to the workshop?"

Again, his question startled her. She looked at Nanette. "Did I return?"

"You did," the needlewoman told her mistress, her tone soothing. "You were very distraught. I found you at Master Bernart's side. You were trying to close his wound with your hands. I had to drag you away from him. I brought you up here while Mistress Gisla remained in the workshop."

Alina's sighed at that. "Aye, you took off my bloodstained gowns and dressed me in these fresh ones."

"Can you tell me where the tally sticks are that Master Bernart was using before he was attacked?" Faucon asked.

His sudden shift of subject caught both women off-guard and left them staring at him, wide-eyed. "Tally sticks?" Mistress Alina asked at last. "What tally sticks?"

"I am but assuming," Faucon offered with a shrug. "It's the way Master Bernart had arranged his coins on the counting board, as if he were calculating wages. I'm surprised that he would do such a chore without also recording to whom and how much he paid."

Again, both women looked startled. Oh aye, something strange was afoot in this house. Mistress Alina was no simple housewife, but an accomplished tradeswoman in her own right, as was Mistress Nanette. It was impossible that they wouldn't know which tools Master Bernart used to do so important a chore. This was especially so with something like the payment of wages, a task that occurred with regularity.

Faucon shook his head, dismissing his question. "It was but a thought. I'm told that Master Bernart had a habit of remaining in the workroom while the household was at its meat."

Mistress Alina pressed her fingers to her temples as if to ease a pain and looked into her lap. His heart sank, sure this was a sign that she was done with him when he wasn't finished with her. He waited for her to either refuse to answer or command him from the room, both of which she had the right to do. She surprised him.

"Your questions are so strange, sir," she said, lifting her head to look at him again. "What does it matter why my husband was in his workroom and not at our table? Is he not still just as dead?"

He followed where she led him, daring to press a little further. "I wish to discern if Peter the Webber knew where Master Bernart would be at this particular hour, and also if he knew that your husband would be alone and unguarded. Aye, and if Peter might have realized he would be able to enter your courtyard and home unseen. Is it possible that others outside your household were aware of your husband's habit of not joining the midday meal?"

"Others? How can I say what others do or do not know?" Alina demanded of Faucon, at last sounding like the powerful mistress of commerce he expected her to be.

"Come now, Mistress," Nanette chided gently, patting Alina's hand as she spoke. "It's no secret, either within these walls or without, that Master Bernart has been avoiding our table for a good while. Say what you know you must. Confirm for Sir Crowner that Peter the Webber knew very well he would find the master alone in his workshop upon the hour of our meal, and that there would be no one to watch his entry into our yard. Also tell him from whom Peter might have learned such a fact."

Alina's expression crumpled at that. Sudden tears glistened in her eyes. She pressed a hand to her mouth, still looking at Nanette.

"You cannot believe that she would have done such a thing?" The words slipped unsteadily between her fingers, more cry than question.

"Who else could have told him?" Nanette replied with a sad shake of her head.

"Nay," Alina moaned, "she wouldn't have. For all that was wrong in Bernart, Gisla loves her sire."

"But I think she loves Peter more," Nanette countered, "and so do you. Her father hurt her deeply when he informed her he was negotiating a marriage contract for her with that Londoner."

Faucon glanced between the women. "You're saying that Mistress Gisla told Peter her father would be alone in the workshop during the household's meal this day?"

"So it would seem," Alina sighed.

Tears slipped unnoticed down her cheeks as she grieved for her daughter the way she didn't mourn her husband. "I have only recently learned that my daughter has been trysting with Peter, doing so against all that is right and proper. Indeed, she may even now be with child by him."

Chapter Seven

The words were both an admission and a dismissal. After offering his condolences, Faucon departed the chamber, leaving Nanette to comfort her mistress as best she could. Descending the stairs, he once more stopped in the doorway of the workshop.

Bernart's body was no longer inside, but the congealed pool of blood that had formed beneath him remained on the floor. Faucon thought the stain left by the merchant's passing would linger long after they removed the gelled mass. Indeed, it was likely that this fine floor would retain the traces of his death for the lifetime of his house.

"Pardon, Sir Faucon," Edmund said from behind him. "I need my desk and the stool."

Faucon stepped aside, allowing his clerk to enter. As Edmund began to gather up his scribing implements, he asked, "Did you receive the widow's oath?"

"I did," Faucon replied.

"Then I can add her name," Edmund said, his back to his master. "I believe we're almost ready for the inquest. The house servants have brought a worktable into the courtyard and placed their master's body upon it. I've asked them to find a second table for Elsa of Stanrudde's body, but they've paid me no heed. I think you'll have to command them to do that, as well as send them to fetch her remains. Lastly, I've found the witnesses we need to testify to the fact of Master Bernart's birth. Perhaps they will also stand as guarantors for the widow."

Here, the monk paused, craning his neck to look at his employer. "Imagine my surprise at discovering we both know one of the men among them."

"We do?" Faucon asked in his own surprise. Neither he nor Edmund hailed from this shire nor had they known one another until two weeks ago. The possibility of coming across any man with whom they were both acquainted was far-fetched indeed.

"Aye. It's that lay brother who assisted us at the miller's death. He was at one of the merchant's homes, treating the children of the house for some ailment or the other," he returned with a brusque and not-at-all approving nod, then went back to packing his basket. Like many Benedictines, Edmund prized his learning the way Bernart had prized his fine house and treasure chests. It wasn't in the clerk to approve of an uneducated man being allowed to join his order.

What irritated Edmund made Faucon grin. Offering no word to his clerk, he turned and exiled into Bernart's courtyard. As Edmund said, the merchant's bloody body now lay on a short wooden worktable, the one that had held Rob's delicate fabric. The table had been placed to one side of the yard where men might file past him with ease, circling around the table to return to the gateway so they could exit. A half-dozen men were gathered behind the corpse. Two of the men wore clothing expensive enough to pronounce them the owners of the nearby homes. Crossing one man's breast was a thick gold chain. The medallion hanging from it bore the town's emblem stamped upon its face, naming him one of the city's aldermen.

Standing next to the worktable, examining the dead merchant, was Brother Colin in his black habit. This day found the former apothecary hatless, exposing his shorn ring of white hair to this afternoon's bright light. Once again, the monk carried his leather pack upon his back, but this time there was no spray of freshly-collected herbs dandling from its top.

"Brother Colin!" Faucon called in greeting, still grinning.

The monk looked up. His dried apple of a face creased even more as he smiled. "Sir Crowner," he called in return.

Colin's pleasure as he once more encountered the shire's Coronarius wasn't reflected on the faces of the men gathered near Bernart. Instead, they watched Faucon with their arms crossed, shoulders squared and expressions wary. As Faucon stopped next to the monk, he offered the man his hand in greeting, as if Colin were a comrade-in-arms rather than a former merchant who now walked a religious path. In truth, Faucon thought of them as equals. Both of them were committed to revealing the hidden tales told by the bodies of dead men. When Brother Colin accepted his hand, the watching townsmen stirred in surprise. Then again, it wasn't often that a Englishman didn't bow to a Norman or that a well-born knight offered a hand to a commoner.

"So how goes your hunt thus far, sir?" the monk asked.

"Very well," Faucon replied with a smile. "This is becoming an interesting chase, when I didn't imagine it could be at first. Yet here I am, only an hour after beginning my task, and already my trail begins to twist and shift in unexpected ways."

Beneath his snowy brows Colin's dark eyes took fire in interest. "Is that so? Then I pray our Lord grants you the time and opportunity to follow it to its rightful end. Should you need a ready ear, I am here."

Faucon choked back his laugh. It was good to know that Colin wasn't beneath begging. Two weeks ago, the monk had served as tutor, schooling his new Crowner in the means and manners of a miller's death. Now he wanted to discover how well his student did in his new vocation, as well as prying out every detail Faucon had gathered thus far about Bernart's passing.

"My thanks, indeed, but I fear you'll need to wait a bit before I have time for conversation. I intend to call the jury in a few moments, hoping to complete the inquest before the moon rises."

Again, the monk's snowy brows lifted. "So soon?"

"What else can I do?" Faucon returned in the pretense of helplessness. "I can hardly wait forty days to conclude this matter if Master Bernart must be buried before that." This seeming fact wasn't precisely true and by Colin's slow smile Faucon saw that the monk knew as much.

Enjoying that Colin stewed, Faucon shifted to face the waiting merchants, ready to introduce himself as he had done so often this day. To his surprise, the men who only moments before had eyed him in something less than welcome now watched him as if he were someone they recognized but couldn't quite remember. Their arms were open and their expressions relaxed.

"Master Manfred, Master Gerard," Colin said, lifting his hand to indicate the better dressed among the men, "this is Sir Faucon de Ramis, or Sir Crowner as he prefers to be called. As of two sennights ago, it is now Sir Crowner's responsibility to hold our inquests. It is also his right to assess and confiscate the king's portion from the estates of those who do murder in our shire."

Faucon shot the monk a startled sidelong look at this last piece. Although Colin's explanation of his duty as assessor was accurate, that part of his position wasn't something Faucon expected to be emphasized, especially not to men who had wealth worthy of royal notice. Apparently Stanrudde's former apothecary knew the folk of his city well indeed. Both merchants smiled and nodded at this. It said that the assessment of estates was another place where Sir Alain had trod too heavily over the years.

"Sir Faucon, Master Manfred is our mercer, bringing us the finest of silks, while Master Gerard deals in fleece like many of the better households in our town. As Brother Edmund requires, both these two masters and their journeymen, here," Colin indicated the four younger men who stood with the merchants, "have lived their whole lives in Stanrudde and have known Master Bernart for all that while. They can swear to the fact of his birth. As can I," he added, "having known Bernart from his earliest days."

"Don't have them speak their words yet," Edmund sang out as he trotted back into the courtyard. He had his desk beneath one arm, the stool hanging from the other and his basket slung by its strap over his shoulder. "I wish to record their names before I hear their vows."

Faucon sighed. It was he, not Edmund, who needed to hear their vows.

The witnesses and Faucon alike watched as Edmund set his stool at the end of Bernart's bier, then carefully laid out the tools he needed at hand: inkpot, quill, whetstone and knife. Edmund placed each implement a precise finger's distance from the next. Then, taking his partially-filled roll of parchment from his basket, he sat on the stool, placed his desk in his lap, and spread the skin atop it.

Once he'd dipped the trimmed end of his quill into the inkpot, he looked expectantly at Faucon. "I'm ready to record the oath of the new widow as first finder."

Faucon nodded and repeated Mistress Alina's words out in the open air where God and the men around him could both bear witness. "Alina of Stanrudde, wife of Bernart le Linsman, swears that she was the first finder, and that she rightfully raised the hue and cry as the law requires."

Then Faucon looked at the two merchants and their

men. "Will you who are Bernart's neighbors, and those men of your household who stand with you today, guarantee on pain of fine that Mistress Alina makes her appearance before the justices when she is called?"

"We will," said Master Gerard, speaking first, the sweep of his hand including the two men who wore the red and green colors of his house.

"Your names?" Edmund asked without lifting his pen or his head.

The wool merchant looked askance at so brusque a command and rude a manner aimed at him by a mere monk. Although the alderman's bearing and the arrangement of his features suggested he was by nature a congenial man, being portly and bald to a fringe of hair around the back of his head, Faucon doubted the merchant was accustomed to such rough treatment.

He smiled at Master Gerard, seeking to soothe the feathers that Edmund had just ruffled. "If you please, master. My clerk and I are ordered by king and court to note all the details of every oath on pain of accruing our own fines. This attention to detail occasionally causes my clerk to be overly rigorous in his routine and his manner."

At Faucon's pretty speech, Edmund lifted his head. The clerk blinked rapidly. "Aye, so it does. My pardon, masters, if I insult. If you will proceed, Sir Faucon? Oh, and don't forget we must yet send men to fetch Elsa of Stanrudde's body."

Faucon swallowed his surprise. Earlier it had been a smile and an attempt to spare his master a fine. Now, a backhanded apology, albeit followed by a command. It was a day for miracles, indeed.

Chapter Eight

With November upon them, the sun's journey across the sky had shortened as winter loomed. Although there was yet another hour before darkness fell and the city gates were closed, around the hour for Vespers, light was already slanting across the courtyard. By the time Edmund had recorded the names and oaths of their witnesses, as well as the facts of Bernart's ancestry, shadows were piling gently around the corners of the merchant's house. At Faucon's command, Bernart's servants found torches, in case the sun set before the jurors had completed their viewing.

One of Master Gerard's journeymen agreed to warn Garret the Weaver, who arrived at Bernart's home soon after, he and his stocky neighbor bringing his mother's body. Elsa was yet wrapped in her tattered blanket. Bernart's servants proved as unwilling to risk fleas as Edmund had been, and claimed no suitable table could be found. At last, Garret laid his mother's body beneath Bernart's bier, then pulled back her blanket to expose her body to God's light against the possibility any juror wished to examine her remains. The two masters sent their other journeymen to carry the call to the parish, alerting the men and all boys over the age of twelve to come.

Unlike peasants in rural villages, who tended to make more solitary treks to the place of a hearing, coming as they did from toft or croft, barn or work shed, these city men arrived as households, some groups as many as thirty strong. Masters strode alongside ancient manservants, apprentices trotted beside those scullery lads who might be of age. Each household pronounced its identity by the color of their garments. There were homes where only blue tunics and red chausses were worn, some where it was green chausses beneath yellow tunics. Faucon eyed one household, garish in its parti-colored tunics of orange and brown, the chausses worn in the opposite arrangement of colors, one leg brown, the other orange.

Households they were and men as well, but that didn't stop them from gossiping like old women. The lurid manner of Bernart's death was shared, man to man and group to group, with everyone along the lane positing his own ideas as to why the merchant might have been killed. As the crowd grew, so did the volume of these suppositions until some men resorted to shouting.

Nor did what should have been a somber gathering prevent the boys from being boys. From one end of the lane a ball, no doubt a sack of dried beans or peas sewn shut, arced its way into the sky. It disappeared into the crowd only to retrace its path a moment later.

Faucon had closed Bernart's gate prior to the jury's arrival, to prevent the men from viewing Bernart's body until they'd given their oaths. Colin now stood on the low exterior wall that lined the lane in front of Bernart's home to monitor the arrivals. At his signal that all the expected households had come, Faucon hoisted himself up next to the monk.

Men and boys packed the rutted earthen path in both directions. To the left—toward the city center, the direction Peter had run when seeking sanctuary—he caught a glimpse of a latecomer appearing out of the jumble of poorer homes, trotting up the lane toward the back of the jury. But when he looked to the right, he breathed out in frustration.

Here, men packed the lane for a dozen or so perches until the pathway bent to the right and disappeared behind a home. How many more waited there, out of sight and, more importantly, out of sound of Bernart's gateway? How could he ever know who among them might not be speaking the words of the vow that bound them to speak the truth, leaving them free to say whatever they may? Although Faucon was certain it was a sin on his part, he didn't wish to leave it up to God to punish those who lied or were foresworn. That task should belong to him.

"I am Sir Crowner, the king's servant in your shire, and I have called this inquest," he shouted.

His words startled a sudden silence from those nearest to him. That abrupt quiet flowed like a steady wave in either direction down the lane. Within the space of a few breaths, all the chatter and hissing ceased, leaving only the distant sound of commerce being transacted at the city's center, punctuated by the ever-present rhythmic clang of smiths working at their anvils. Nearby, a rooster crowed, calling his hens home for the night. Singing their harsh rasping song, the swallows nesting in the eaves of the linsman's warehouse darted and circled over Faucon's head, seeking that last fly before retiring.

"You are here this day in the matter of two deaths, that of Bernart le Linsman and Elsa of Stanrudde, a weaver," he shouted, scanning as many among the crowd as he could see. "As you give your oath, know that it binds you before God to speak the truth, should you be asked to give any information about either death. Your oath also binds you to speak truthfully if you are asked for information regarding the property of the one who killed Master Bernart. Swear now that you will deny the verdict of murder in the matter of Elsa of Stanrudde, who passed instead because our Lord called her to Him, and confirm the verdict of murder for Bernart le Linsman."

"Wait!" someone bellowed. "This new Crowner is not speaking the words as he must."

Every last man and boy in the crowd looked in the direction of the call, the rustle of their movement echoing loudly around the lane. It was Hodge the Pleykster. The big man was pushing his way through the back of the crowd, working his way forward as if he meant to claim a spot at Bernart's gate. Against the better-dressed among this crowd, he looked out of place in his splotched tunic and apron. "He must ask you to confirm that Peter the Webber is the man who killed Bernart," the man who bleached the linen for Bernart shouted as he came.

Faucon grimaced at the challenge, one he should have expected, given the hue and cry, but hadn't considered he might face. He raised his hand, ready to call for the watching jurors to part so Hodge could reach the gateway. If God was good, he might be able to woo the man into compliance with private conversation.

Before he could speak, a dark and dangerous sound rose from a household on the opposite end of the lane. These men wore parti-colored tunics of dark green and a blue pale enough to remind Faucon of Bernart's colors.

"He doesn't belong here. Robert, you and yours hold him! Do not let him pass!" shouted a long, lanky man from the middle of that household.

At his hoarse command, the group of men all dressed in red and yellow linked arms and shifted, forming a barricade across the lane, trapping the pleykster behind them.

"You cannot stop me, Roger, not even if you call every household who owes you favors to do your bidding," Hodge returned at the same angry volume, now trapped behind that wall of men. "Your son murdered my friend, and everyone within our city walls knows it. This inquest jury must confirm it."

Roger and his household all howled at that, every man among them crying that their master's son was innocent. Fists clenched, they surged forward, carving their own path through those between them and the man they meant to attack. Up and down the lane, jurors began to choose sides, either for or against Peter, each side shouting out their accusations and proofs to the other.

Faucon groaned. Not only had he lost his opportunity to soothe Hodge, his inquest was about to become a battlefield. "In the king's name I command you to cease!" he bellowed, drawing his sword and holding it out before him.

"Peace, all of you!" Brother Colin added from beside him, to no avail.

"The guard comes!" those jurors standing behind Hodge began to shout.

As the cry was carried from mouth to mouth and man to man, everywhere along the lane jurors opened their fists and dropped into a disappointed silence. Two dozen city soldiers in their green tunics made their way out of the city center and toward the jury at a fast pace. At their head was a dark-haired man, this soldier dressed in brown rather than green with a leather hauberk–the sort of armor worn by the common soldiers who earned their bread with their swords–atop his tunic. To further confound the issue, this leader who dressed like a common soldier wore a knight's long sword.

Those in the lane behind Hodge shifted this way and that, allowing the troop to pass. As the guardsmen reached the pleykster, they formed a circle around him, whether to restrain or protect him, there was no saying. Once Hodge was secure, their leader left them, continuing forward through the crowd toward Bernart's gate. Grateful for this unexpected intervention, Faucon made a show of sheathing his sword as he again scanned the crowd.

"Aye, this may not be how inquests have been prosecuted in the past," he shouted, only hoping all could hear. "But change is the purpose for my election and my new position as your Crowner. You all know that Peter the Webber has claimed sanctuary. Thus, you also know that the time for accusation and arrest remains forty days hence, when by law he must exit the church. Now, on this day and at this time, I ask only that the men of this jury view Master Bernart's body and declare him murdered."

Hodge, trapped in the encircling guard, made a frantic noise. "This is wrong," he shouted. "This Crowner must name the man who killed Bernart. If he will not, then we should call for Sir Alain. Our sheriff knows how this must be done."

"Call for him as you may," Faucon replied, not addressing Hodge directly as he scanned the watching men. "But if you do, make no mistake. Sir Alain will only say the same to you, that I, who am the Servant of the Crown for this shire, have the right to hold your inquests, doing so in the manner that the law and our king requires."

Only then, did Faucon look directly at Hodge. His stomach soured. What he next said would likely cheat him of the opportunity to speak with the pleykster in any way save hostile confrontation. This, when Faucon was certain he needed the merchant disarmed and open to his questions. But, right now, it was vital to establish his rights and privileges as Crowner.

"Master Pleykster, I am told that Stanrudde pays the king so that inquest juries are drawn only from the parish in which an assault occurred. If you are not of this parish, then you are not required to attend this inquest. Stay as you will, but if you stay you may only confirm the verdict as I command."

Giving the man no chance to respond, Faucon repeated, "Men of Stanrudde, do you swear to confirm the verdict of murder in the death of Bernart the Linsman and that of natural death for the weaver Elsa? Do you swear to speak the truth if asked for any information or assessments in either matter?"

"I so swear!" Each man's individual oath tangled with the next to become a roar of sound that reverberated as high as Heaven itself.

Hodge threw back his head, his eyes shut. When he pivoted, the town guard turned with him. Maintaining their circle around him, they escorted him out of the crowd and back the way he'd come.

"Then enter and view the bodies as you must," Faucon shouted to all who remained, watching Hodge leave, knowing the man took with him precious bits of information that he might never discover.

Chapⱦer nine

Bernart's servants opened the gate. Still fretting over the opportunity he was sure he'd lost, Faucon looked at the soldier who had led the town guard. The dark-haired man had pressed forward to the head of the crowd until he stood to one side of Bernart's gate, watching the other jurors enter past him.

Faucon blinked, and looked again, certain he was mistaken. This soldier was bearded, brown of eye and hair, and older than Faucon by more than a decade. He was built much like Faucon, being broad of shoulder, thick of arm and narrow of hip. A new scar drew a fine line down one side of his rawboned face, and his strong nose bore a slight crook, the result of a long ago break. Indeed, a ten-year-old break. It had happened when this man and one of his younger half-brothers had fought over a family matter.

"Temric of Graistan?" Faucon asked in astonishment, clambering down off the wall.

At Faucon's call, the man joined the crowd long enough to step inside Bernart's courtyard, then exited the flow to stand with his Crowner. He bowed, offering the greeting of commoner to noble, rather than meeting Faucon as knights did, by clasping hands. Then again, Temric, Bastard of Graistan, was a knight who had refused his title and chose instead to serve his younger brother, Lord Graistan, as a simple master-at-arms, a commoner's position.

"Aye, that is who I am, Sir Faucon," Temric replied,

not sounding particularly pleased at their unexpected meeting. Then again, Faucon had never heard this strange man sound pleased about anything.

"Why are you leading the town guard?" Faucon asked, still reeling over the coincidence of their meeting.

"I don't lead the guard," Temric replied, unconsciously settling into a warrior's stance, his hand resting on the hilt of his sword. "But I have been helping their master train the younger journeymen. It just so happened I was on the practice yard when the lad arrived, saying that this inquest was afoot and that the pleykster meant to interfere." Here he stopped, when Faucon craved more.

"But why are you in Stanrudde at all?" he persisted in confusion.

"My mother lives here. She's recently widowed and begged my presence and assistance so she may grieve as she must. As her house is in this parish, I am one of your jurors. So here I am," replied the man who was both English and Norman at once. His lips twisted into a tight and crooked smile. "I might ask the same of you, Sir Faucon. How come you to be in Stanrudde, acting as this Crowner?"

Faucon laughed at that. "At your lord brother's command," he replied. "Bishop William was determined to force Lord Graistan to take on these new duties, while Lord Rannulf was just as determined not to be forced where he didn't wish to go. To save himself, he raised my name and threw me to the wolves."

Grinning, Faucon added, "Not that I am complaining, mind you. To hold this position a knight must have an income of twenty pounds a year, which bishop and baron together have made mine. That and Blacklea Village," he added.

"Blacklea Village?" Brother Colin murmured from

beside Faucon, having descended from the wall to join them. "I once knew a man from that place." There was a note of sadness in his comment.

Faucon opened his mouth to introduce the monk to the soldier, but before he could speak, Temric nodded to Colin.

"Brother, it is good to see you again. You look well."

"As do you, Richard Alwynason," Colin replied, smiling at the soldier.

Faucon almost gaped. In all the time he'd known Temric, the man had never allowed anyone to use his proper name, not even his brothers. Especially not his brothers.

"How does Master Jehan these days?" Colin was asking. "He's refused to see me since I dared tell him he'd not regain his legs after that fall of his."

All the life left Temric's face, his mouth settling into a grim line, suggesting there was little love lost between this master and the soldier. "He does well enough. Although he doesn't yet walk, he does ride now. He and my mother went together to collect the last of the fleece due them, sparing me the travel. If you will excuse me?" He took a backward step. "I'll do my duty to our king and be on with my day as I must."

"Wait, Temric," Faucon said, calling him back. "I've not seen my cousins in a good while. Might I beg an hour of your time this evening after all is complete here? Will you join me and share what news you have of them?"

Emotions flashed across the soldier's face, not the least of which was reluctance. But a lifetime of service to those he'd placed above him won out. Temric nodded. "As you will, Sir Faucon. There's an alewife's shop near the city center, if that suits."

Faucon grinned at that. "Aye, I think I know the place. I caught a wondrous smell as I came in this direction."

That made Colin laugh while Temric managed a small smile. "Aye, he found the place," the monk said. "I'll come with him, Richard, to show him the way. Shall we call at Mistress Alwyna's house to collect you, once Sir Crowner is free?"

Temric gave a quick shake of his head at that. "There's no need. Come to the alewife's house when you are ready and you'll find me there awaiting you. I'll see that she saves aside both stew and brew for you."

As Temric moved past Faucon to do his duty as a juror, Roger the Webber started inside the gate, his household at his back. Although an alderman's gold chain crossed his breast, Peter's father seemed more a laborer—like a man who worked with his hands and enjoyed doing so—than the other rich merchants in the crowd, who looked more barons than townsmen. His face was time-seamed and summer-browned, his light brown hair streaked with gold from exposure to the sun. Clean-shaven, his cheekbones were high and sharp, and his nose bony. His blue eyes seemed all the brighter against his sun-darkened skin.

The webber radiated anger, his jaw tight and his eyes narrowed. His men followed inside Bernart's gate at a strut, their fists yet clenched in the promise of violence, as if daring any and all to once again suggest Peter's guilt. Stopping in front of Faucon, the master bowed, his movement so stiff it seemed as if he might shatter in twain as he made it.

Faucon glanced at the webber's shoes. His feet were wider and longer—longer than Faucon would have expected for a man of his height—than the mark on the floor. Although Roger wore footwear of a better quality than that Rob and Tom owned, the man's shoes were coated with the same mud and manure as theirs. There was no sign of blood.

"Sir Crowner," Peter's father said, his words clipped and tight. "I am here to avow that my son is innocent of

Bernart's death. When the day comes that he is called to stand before the justices I will bring forty men—nay! I will bring a hundred men to swear to his innocence. No other man will be able to bring as many, and you and your justices will be forced to clear my son's name of this wrongful charge. You will not take him from me!" His voice rose with every word as he threw his challenge like a glove. It was a father's promise to fight to the death to save his son's life.

Faucon opened his mouth to reply, but Colin was there before him. "As you should do, Roger. As would any loving father do for his only son," the monk told him, stepping forward to put his hand on the webber's arm. "Hear me, Roger. Sir Crowner is not our sheriff. Do not wait to sway the justices with your witnesses on some day long hence when they arrive at last. Help our crowner today. You say Peter is innocent. Then here is the man to prove this to everyone within our town walls," he said, lifting a hand to indicate Faucon. "The truth is all our Crowner seeks. Know that if he can assure himself Peter was not the one to kill Bernart, he will do more than clear Peter's name. He will find the man who did this deed and see him arrested in Peter's place."

The webber drew a sharp breath at this. He glanced from Colin to his Crowner. An instant later, his shoulders relaxed and his brow cleared.

As Colin saw bravado drain from the webber, he patted the man's arm, then shifted to the side, once again reclaiming his role as an observer. The monk shot Faucon a swift glance as he did so, offering a shrug of apology for intruding. It was a wholly unnecessary gesture.

"Master Webber," Faucon said, offering Roger a nod as if nothing had gone between them in the prior moment. "I am grateful I was in Stanrudde on this day to attend to your son in his distress. I hope that you can take some comfort in knowing Peter is safe and well-guarded for the moment."

Roger's eyes closed. He dragged his fingers through his hair. "God save my son," he muttered in private prayer.

When he opened his eyes again, he looked at the men of his household. "Go you. View yon bitch's son and pronounce him murdered, a fate he well deserved. Then get you back to our house and your tasks. We've wasted time enough today. You've all got flax to break so we can make our deliveries on the morrow as we always do."

Although yet grumbling and muttering in defense of their master's son, the men of Roger's household did as they were commanded, moving on to fulfill their duty to court and king.

Faucon offered Peter's father a quick smile. "As Colin has said, I'm committed to discovering who killed Bernart. If I'm to do that, then you must answer my questions and do so honestly. Will you speak to me of the planned union between your son and Bernart's daughter?"

"What union?" the merchant retorted, his words bitter and his eyes narrowed. "Three months ago, what I thought settled between my house and this one, yon dead oath-breaker made disappear with a snap of his fingers."

Faucon nodded. "So Mistress Alina tells me. She also says there was never a contract between your houses. How is it possible that you might have arranged such a union without one?" he asked in true confusion.

Roger once more dragged his fingers through his hair, this time pausing to scrub at the back of his neck as if to ease an ache. "'What need have we for scribing,' Bernart says to me," the webber mocked, his scorn aimed at himself, "'what with us having been friends for all our lives?' More fool me, because I *have* known Bernart all my life. Oh aye, I'd seen him use others in this same way, but I never believed he would do me so." He paused to sigh. "Not me. We were like brothers, or so I thought."

"So there truly is no contract?" Faucon persisted.

"Do you think me an idiot?" Roger retorted, with far more heat than was warranted. "Nay, nothing was scribed, but we had an agreement, spoken before witnesses." The merchant gave a harsh laugh at that. "Didn't both his household and mine come together on that auspicious day? Indeed, Bernart and his own sat at my tables and drank my wine as we celebrated the future nuptials of our children."

That made Faucon frown. It was one thing for a seducer to promise marriage to a woman beneath the sky with none but the stars to witness. Such an agreement was as empty as the air that heard the words, and a woman foolish to believe her lover's vows. It was quite another to make that same promise when a crowd marked what was spoken between the agreeing parties. Aye, there were some men in this world who understood the mystery of the written word, but they were mostly monks. Faucon had once grasped some of that skill, but after his brother's accident he'd happily forgotten all, consumed by the joy of learning a warrior's trade. But because so many men in this world had no knowledge of that mystery, an oath or spoken agreement was as precious and as valid to them as anything Edmund scratched onto his parchment.

"I'm told there was no betrothal ceremony either," Faucon said. "I can't understand why Mistress Gisla and your son didn't trade vows after you and Bernart came to your agreement." That was the usual way of such unions, the two households settling on dower and dowry, then the young couple sharing the vows of betrothal to confirm that the marriage would occur at some point in the future. "That would have affirmed your promises and made the union between your children almost unbreakable."

Something akin to shame washed over Roger's face. "When this all began, we had planned for our babes to wed within a month or two after we came to terms. Peter was to have come live here as Bernart's journeyman, learning what Bernart could teach him. Hence, there was no reason for the trading of such vows, or so Bernart assured me. But almost immediately the delays began, this month Bernart saying that Gisla was too young for marriage, the next saying that Alina wasn't ready to share her house with a strange lad or another married woman."

Here, the merchant stopped to bow his head, no longer able to meet Faucon's gaze. "God help me, perhaps I am an idiot," he said quietly, "blinded by my own greed for what Bernart offered. Today, I know that it wasn't Alina delaying the wedding, it was that bitch's son stalling, waiting for a better offer and hiding behind his wife and daughter as he did."

"Still, the promises you had between the two of you should have served even without the betrothal," Faucon said. "Why not bring a complaint against Bernart for breaking his end of your agreement?"

The webber straightened with a start to glare at his Crowner. "What good would that do?" he snapped. "Gisla would have been wedded and bedded, and most likely have brought forth her first child, before your royal justices ever saw my complaint, much less ruled on it. Damn Bernart! He added insult to injury when he came offering me coins to convince me to let him break his oath. As if his coins could heal the wrong he'd done to me and my house! I threw his purse back at him."

He sighed, then continued in a softer voice. "What else could I do? My son has fixed his heart on Gisla and

SEASON OF THE FOX

will not be moved."

"Ah," Faucon said, then hesitated, for what followed was a delicate subject to explore, especially with Peter's father. "I'm told that your son and Gisla have taken the matter of their union into their own hands and are trysting. Is this true?"

Shock started through Roger's blue eyes. He gaped at Faucon, his face the image of astonishment. Then surprise ebbed and wicked amusement took its place.

"By God, is that so? Well, Peter hoodwinked me for certain. I had no idea." He laughed, his face creasing even further with the depth of his pleasure. "Now, wouldn't that have tweaked Bernart right smartly if his proud London merchant had thrown back his daughter as damaged goods?"

Still nodding in satisfaction at the vengeance his son had dealt his former friend, Roger continued, "Well now, I begin to think Bernart's passing is all to my good. Once Peter has been adjudged innocent, I'll see Alina fulfills our contract and we'll get the two wed before any little bastard sees the light of day."

Faucon wasn't as certain of that outcome as Roger. "So, tell me of Peter's doings this day. When did he leave your house? Where did he tell you was he going?"

"He left this morning and told me nothing of where he went, because, as far as I knew, he was going where he always did," Roger replied. "My son is a journeyman like all the others in my house. Every day Peter takes broken flax to those spinners he manages, so they might turn it into thread, collecting from them what they've finished. Depending on Mistress Alina's needs, he then takes the new thread to the dyers for coloring or takes raw thread to the weavers with whom we work. It's the job of my journeymen to string the weavers' looms for each piece, instructing them on what pattern, if any, is to be produced. When a weaver finishes a piece, it's on my journeymen to remove the completed project, so the weaver bears no fault should something go amiss in that process."

Here the webber paused. The jerk of his chin indicated Garret, who squatted next to his mother's body as the men of the jury made their steady passage around the table. "He's one of ours," Roger said. "Upon Bernart's return from his last trip to London, he was eager to begin creating the wimples that the high-born ladies are all wanting to wear these days. Both Garret and his mother proved adept at weaving the delicate cloth needed for such pieces. More's the pity that she's gone. She was a good weaver and faster than he. Now I'll not only be short what she made, but be getting half as much from him. Elsa kept him working and away from his ale."

In his memory, Faucon again saw the airy drift of fabric off of Rob's table as he entered Bernart's courtyard. Unlike the usual warm cream color of raw linen, this fabric had been snow white. "Does Peter take that fine stuff to the pleykster after he retrieves it from his weavers?" he asked, certain what the answer would be.

"Aye, it goes to Hodge." Roger's voice broke. He cursed beneath his breath. When he again looked at Faucon, honest confusion and deep hurt filled his gaze. He shook his head like one befuddled.

"Two of the men I once held most dear in my life, lost to me in the space of three months. They have both known my son from the day of his birth. How could either one have set his heart against Peter? Nor can I understand how Hodge would accuse my son of slaying Bernart when he knows my lad as well as I do. No matter what wrong Bernart might have done, to me, to my son, to a beggar on the street or Christ Himself, Peter would never have killed the man who was his future wife's father."

He shifted, his hands once again closed into fists as

he boldly met Faucon's gaze. "I would have. By God, I should have killed Bernart the day he broke our agreement. He deserved no less. But, Peter? Nay, never Peter, I know it, aye."

With that, Roger's arrogance and anger returned, he straightened to his tallest, then looked down his thin nose at his Crowner. "Have you any further questions for me?"

"Not at this moment," Faucon replied with a smile. "But more may occur as time passes."

Roger gave a brusque nod. "Seek me out if you have need, sir. For the now, I and mine have work to attend."

Without waiting for Faucon's response, the webber pivoted and walked toward the table on which Bernart lay.

Chapter Ten

Faucon watched as the master webber paused next to Bernart's body and spat into the dirt at the table leg before moving on. "What say you?" he asked Colin quietly.

"That Roger is a very angry man," the monk replied, still watching the webber. "As he has every right to be, if what he says is true. But I fear he has no excuse for what happened to him in regard to that contract. He knew Bernart better than any man. Save Hodge, I suppose," he added.

That stirred Faucon's interest. "So Bernart has been an oath-breaker all his life? If that's so, why did his former master put so much stock in him that he wed him to his daughter?"

Colin smiled at that. "Sir Crowner, if you wish to understand these men, you must learn to think like them. Master William chose Bernart for Alina because Bernart was brilliant at turning pretty ribbons into silver. No matter to whom that lad spoke, his manner was friendly, his words were always honey, and his attitude respectful but never fawning. It was the exact concoction needed to induce the wellborn folk who became Mistress Elinor's customers, and Mistress Alina's after her, to buy more than they intended. It's a skill that neither William nor his other two apprentices could master."

The monk lifted a hand to indicate the proud house. "As you can see, it worked quite well for Bernart, at least until now. Have you time to share what you've learned with me? Might I see where Bernart died?"

"Of course," Faucon replied. "And I'm more than grateful for any insight you can offer."

Waving to Edmund so his clerk knew he was stepping away, Faucon led Colin to Bernart's workroom. A bucket of water now stood in the doorway, a short-bristled broom and a pot of soap at its side. Inside, a pair of lasses, no doubt the girls who now swept ashes from the hearth in Nanette's place, knelt on the stone floor as far as possible from the spot where their master died. The two were half-heartedly plying their wet rags on tiles that were already clean.

Faucon's heart jumped as his gaze flew to the shadow print. It was still there. He added yet another note on his mental list of mistakes not to make a second time. There would be no cleaning at the site of a death until he gave permission that it be done.

"Give us a moment, my dears," Colin said to the lasses.

The alacrity with which they tossed aside their rags and fled said neither wished to touch their dead master's spilled blood. As if to prove that point, they both shot a glance at the far end of the chamber and crossed themselves as they departed.

Entering the room ahead of Faucon, Colin went to crouch near the gruesome puddle. "He lay here as he bled his last, I see," the monk said, then looked more closely at the gelled and seeping remains of Bernart's life. He shifted in his crouch, his gaze wide-eyed. "But the hue and cry was–"

"Exactly so," Faucon interrupted with a grin, then stepped into the clean area that had been beneath Bernart's stool, shifting into the murderer's stance. He lifted his arms, his hands poised as if he were about to slice through the merchant's neck. "Bernart was sitting here on his stool when he was attacked."

He mimed the act of murder, then stepped back to

once more frown down at the counting board. Every one of the coins still sat where it had been when he'd entered the workshop. That was unexpected, considering that the whole parish was now in the courtyard and the workshop was more or less unguarded. Serving lasses were hardly a deterrent to theft. Perhaps this was just the way those were who had as much wealth as Bernart, that a few stained coins were of little matter.

"Come look at this, Brother," he said to Colin. "You were once a man of commerce. Tell me what you see upon this board."

The monk joined his Crowner and stared down at the blood-spattered coins on the board for a moment. "Many small payments. Perhaps the sums he owed for the minor things a household needs day-to-day?" As soon as the words were out Colin shook his head. "Nay, that cannot be. There are too many stacks with the same number of coins in them. These are wages."

"My thought as well," Faucon replied, "although neither Mistress Alina nor Mistress Nanette were able to confirm that for me."

The monk's brows rose at that. Faucon nodded. "Again, exactly my reaction. Now tell me this. When you were a man of the world, would you have calculated the sums you owed men, whether for goods or services, with your tally sticks and purse yet locked into your treasure chest?"

The surprise on Colin's face deepened. "Never," came his stout reply.

As Faucon had done before him, the monk turned to scan the chests in the workroom. "All locked? And they were like this when you first entered?"

"Aye, nothing's changed since I arrived just after the hue and cry chased Peter into his sanctuary." He paused, shifting his bits and pieces as he thought. "I cannot make sense of it. Why put away the tally sticks and purse, but not remove the coins from the board?"

"Perhaps the one putting away these things intended to collect the coins as well, only to be interrupted by Peter's arrival?" Colin offered.

Faucon shook his head at that. "I think not. Peter's arrival was no interruption. It was intended and well-timed. Here, look at this," he said, stepping back and pointing to the shadow print on the floor.

Colin came to stand at his side. He stared in silence at the area of tile Faucon indicated for an instant, then shot a sidelong look at his Crowner. "What am I looking at?"

That made Faucon laugh. "Not one for the hunt, are you?"

"Never in my life," the monk admitted, smiling. "I'm a city man, born and bred."

Making a show of it, Faucon eased the toe of his soft leather boot into the clear spot, until the print became a bare outline of clean floor around his foot, making the shape clear.

"A shoe!" the monk cried out. "He left a trace!"

"He did, indeed," Faucon replied, then crouched to once again place his hand into the clean area, refreshing his memory of its outline. "What you see here isn't the spoor of just any man bent on dealing out death. Nay, the one who did this deed was so trusted that he was able to walk up behind Bernart and ply half of a strange scissors across the man's throat before Bernart even knew what he was about. All I need do now is find a man beloved by Bernart who wears one shoe spattered with blood."

"I take it that man is not Roger," Colin remarked, coming to crouch next to his Crowner.

"Hardly so." Faucon traced the outline with his finger. "Even if the webber hadn't worn a shoe clean of gore, I would have known it wasn't he who did this. He loves his son too deeply, that one. He'd never use his child to shield his own wrongdoing. So, who did Bernart love that much and who loved him in return? Hodge is a name that comes, for he grieved mightily at the hue and cry."

"Aye, so Hodge might do, but he's not a man Bernart ever betrayed," Colin replied, shaking his head to emphasize his certainty. "Indeed, now that Roger is betrayed, Hodge may be the only man left in Stanrudde whose fingers Bernart never burnt."

As Faucon opened his mouth to speak, Colin held up a forestalling hand. "Don't misinterpret nor take any heed of my opinion. All I'm saying is that I cannot imagine him wishing his friend dead. To me, this act has the look of vengeance to it, and I see no reason for Hodge to revenge himself on Bernart."

"Say what you will, Brother, and I'll be grateful for it," Faucon replied. "All I intended to say was that I saw Hodge at the church where Peter has gone to ground. He's a tall man and this shoe suggests someone smaller."

"Ah," Colin replied. "Well then, I'll say that I think the question you'd best ask is who once loved Bernart that much, then was betrayed. I'll warn you. The numbers could be legion. Bernart couldn't prevent himself from using others any more than a fish can stop swimming. It was a bad habit that grew steadily worse once he began living like a lord."

"If that's so, then why did so many men of the hue and cry scream for Peter's blood, behaving as if Bernart were their own brother?" Faucon protested.

That made the monk laugh. "They don't love Bernart any more than they love anyone else. All you saw was men enjoying the chase, sir, just as you do. Once they were on Peter's trail, they raced after him, longing to taste blood at the hunt's end."

"More fool me," Faucon replied, laughing at his own blindness. "In my own defense, I'll tell you I'm the sort of hunter who cares naught if I return with prey in hand or leave the creature standing where I've cornered it, so I might chase it again another day."

"Is that so?" Colin replied, looking surprised, then gave a jerk of his head to indicate the print on the floor. "Why not make a pattern?"

Faucon shot him a startled sidelong glance. "I beg your pardon?"

"A pattern. We're at a linsman's house. Perhaps the workmen have a scrap of fabric. If we press it on the floor, it's possible the dried blood will leave an outline."

That made Faucon grin in excitement. "I never thought! I know just the men with the skill to do that for me. Give me a moment," he told Colin, coming to his feet, "and don't let those lasses back in to do their work while I'm gone."

"As you command, sir," Colin agreed with a laugh.

Hurrying across the merchant's yard to the storehouse, Faucon found Rob and Tom sitting on a table just inside the door. With them were another half-dozen of Bernart's manservants and laborers. As they had already made their circuit around the table as part of the jury, they were now watching their betters and neighbors parade past their dead master.

"Have you found the bolt to your scissors?" he asked Rob.

The shy man glanced at him, then swiftly away. "I have not, sir, but Tom says our new mistress won't take the value of that bolt from my wages," he replied in relief. "We did search as much of the floor in the workshop as we could. We weren't wont to move any of the chests, not without the mistress's permission. It is not so large a thing, that bolt. Perhaps it rolled beneath one of them."

"Possibly," Faucon agreed although he no longer believed they would find what Rob sought in the workshop. Nay, he was convinced he'd find that bolt in the purse of the one who had opened the scissors. "Are your hands as steady with a tool that's not as sharp as your scissors, Rob?"

Tom lifted his brows at the question. "Indeed, they are, sir," he answered for his brother. "What is it you want Rob to do?"

A few moments later, the two laborers were back in the workshop, both of them crouching near their master's worktable, a scrap of linen in Tom's hand. Rob had brought with him a pot of ground charcoal. Using the tip of his smallest finger, he carefully spread the smut at the outer edge of the clean area, then took the fabric Tom held. Drawing it taut between his hands, he painstakingly pressed it to the floor inside the shape. When he was satisfied, he lifted the scrap to show his Crowner how the charcoal had marked the cloth.

"Does this suit, sir?" he asked.

When Faucon nodded, Tom handed him a more typical pair of shears, one made in the usual way, as a continuous piece of metal looped to form cutting blades. Lifting the cloth to what light yet streamed in through the windows, Rob clipped slowly and carefully along the outside of the mark, proving his worth. A moment later, he placed the shaped scrap into the print. It fit perfectly.

Faucon and Colin both grinned as they studied it. "Exactly a shoe," the monk said to Rob, "or rather, most of one. Well done, lad."

Colin nodded to Faucon. "Now, Sir Crowner, all you need do is take this around to Stanrudde's shoemakers. I wager one of them will have a form that matches this shape."

Once again, the monk's suggestion caught Faucon by surprise. This was a far easier route to discovering the owner of that foot, and by far a better way to follow his trail to the solution he now craved. "And here I envisioned myself walking the lanes in town, staring at every man's shoes," he laughed, then shook his head at Colin. "I see there remains much for me to learn about this sort of hunting. So, how many shoemakers are there in this town?"

"Four," all three men replied as one.

"But only two of them are true craftsmen," Colin added.

That made Rob and Tom hoot. "You still hold affection for your parish, Brother," Tom said in mock complaint.

"That's possible," Colin said with a grin, then looked at Faucon. "Why do you ask, Sir Crowner?"

"If there are four, then I wonder if Rob might make me three more copies of this pattern, so each shoemaker could have one to compare to his own patterns that he holds in store. Would you, Rob?"

"Aye, I can do that," the shy man replied, holding Faucon's precious scrap.

"My thanks. It's a great boon you're doing me," he said, then glanced between the men, considering asking them to guard their tongues about what they'd done for him. He instantly dismissed the idea as futile. No matter what vow he had from them, their tongues would surely wag. The whole household would soon know their Crowner had asked them to make that pattern, and that he'd found something of import in the workshop.

"Would either of you know where I might find Mistress Gisla?" he asked instead.

"Aye," Tom said. "She said she couldn't bear to watch the jury, so she took the hogs back to their pen, then went to the far end of the garden." He pointed to the west, in the direction of the kitchen, to show them where he meant. "I expect you'll find her on the bench we keep back there, under the apple trees. She likes it there because it's private and quiet." As he said this, the workman winked.

Oh aye, tongues wagged in this household. Faucon guessed there wasn't a man, woman or child within these walls who didn't know that their young mistress had been meeting illicitly with Peter.

Thanking the man again, Faucon turned for the door when a thought struck him. He looked back at the brothers. "Tell me this, if you can. Did Mistress Alina leave the table more than once to urge your master to join you at your meat?"

It was Rob who answered, doing so with certainty. "Aye, sir. She went three times."

"Only three? Are you sure?" Tom countered.

Rob nodded, then cast his gaze downward again. "I am. She went fewer times than usual."

His brother gave a harsh laugh. "Aye, fewer times for sure, but that was only because the master came up dead on her third trip down."

"How long was she gone from the table on each visit?" Faucon wanted to know.

Tom squinted up at him. "Usually she's gone only as long as it takes her to speak the words, reminding the master it's time for him to join us. But this day, she stayed a goodly while as she made that second trip down the stairs. I think it was because she argued with the master. Is that not right, Rob?"

His brother nodded in agreement.

"But you didn't hear them arguing?" Faucon asked in surprise.

It was Rob who answered. "The floor between hall and workshop is stone. You cannot hear anything, not if yon door is closed." He indicated the workshop door.

"So how long do you think she remained in here on that second trip?" Faucon pressed. "As long as it might take her to go into your kitchen, say? Or perhaps farther than that? It's not necessary to be exact. I'm but conjuring how this all happened. It helps me to know the particulars," he added, to assure the men he asked nothing untoward of them, nothing that might threaten the livelihoods they made for themselves here.

Rob said nothing. Tom glanced from his Crowner to the monk. Colin smiled at him, nodding to encourage an answer. The workman eased back on his heels and closed his eyes for a moment as he thought.

"By my steps, I think she was gone as long as it would take me to pace slowly twice around our storehouse," he replied as he opened his eyes.

"Did anyone else leave the table before your master died?" It was Colin who asked this question.

"Mistress Nanette," Rob said to the floor. "She went to the kitchen, wanting milk instead of our usual ale."

Startled, Faucon stared at the laborer. As an acknowledged mistress in her trade, Nanette was no different than Gisla or Alina. If she wanted a cup of milk, she could ask one of her apprentices or any other servant in the house to do the task for her. "She went for it herself? Why?"

Once again, the men sent him that look, the one empty of all save surprise that a knight such as he would pose them that question. Since it wasn't really the answer he needed, Faucon rephrased.

"When did Mistress Nanette go to the kitchen? Before or after the mistress's second trip down here?"

"Before," said Rob while Tom answered in the same instant, "After."

"After," Tom insisted, looking at his brother. "Remember how Mistress Alina came back after that second time and how upset she was? She was wringing her hands and almost crying. They nearly collided as Mistress Nanette came to her feet with her cup in her hand. That's when Mistress Nanette spoke aloud of how much she preferred milk to ale."

He looked at Faucon. "Mistress Nanette made a show of her words. It's something she always does after the master has upset the mistress. I think she believes it distracts us from noticing the master's cruelty toward his wife," he finished, his tone suggesting Nanette's efforts were wasted.

"How long was Mistress Nanette gone?" Faucon asked.

Tom shrugged. "No longer than it took her to fill her cup and return, I suppose. I wasn't paying any heed to her comings and goings. I'm not certain if she returned to the hall. I think she might have been just outside the hall door when Mistress Alina again passed her, making that last trip down to the workshop to convince the master to come to the table. But he couldn't come join us, could he?" the man said. "Not with him just then made dead by Master Peter's hand. That's when the mistress stirred us all to the hue and cry."

Faucon offered them a grateful nod. "My thanks. You have been a great help, indeed."

Chapter Eleven

A
s he and Colin left the house, Faucon led the way across the courtyard to the storehouse. "I take it we are walking," the monk said.

"We are," Faucon replied. "After that, if you don't mind, perhaps you'll come with me to speak to Mistress Gisla. I'm hoping she'll better tolerate my presence and answer truthfully if you're at my side."

"Of course," Colin replied as they started on their first trip around the storehouse.

Faucon chose a pace he imagined slow to a servant who didn't care much for his master. When he and Colin crossed their starting point for the second time, he looked at the monk. "I say that's long enough to stand behind a man, slash his throat, then return his tally sticks and purse to a chest. What say you?"

"I say you're right about that, but I think it's not long enough for that same person to also clean away the blood that surely stained her hands as well as a single shoe. Or to change her gown which must have been befouled after such slaughter."

"Her, is it now?" Faucon laughed.

Colin shot him a quizzical look at that. "Why ask about Mistress Alina's whereabouts if you're not thinking she did this?"

"I'm not certain what I think yet," Faucon replied. "That's not true. I'm certain of one thing. Peter the Webber did not kill Bernart. So, if not to do murder, why was he in the workroom? I suspect I know why, but I crave confirmation from the one he came to see, among other things."

Starting in the direction of the garden behind the kitchen, he cast an eye to the heavens above him. At the western horizon, the setting sun shot hazy rays of light through a now orange and pink sky, while to the east, hints of twilight's deep blue began to stain what remained of the day's clouds. As if drawing strength from the shift of light to dark, the breeze stirred anew, its breath now filled with the crisp chill of an autumn night.

The structure in which the household's meals were prepared was about a third the size of the house. When Faucon had first stepped into the courtyard, there'd been only a narrow trail of smoke lazily twining skyward from its smoke hole. Now, a thick twisting rope of fragrant air pooled above its thatched roof. Nanette's charges were hard a-work, creating a feast for the master's wake upon the morrow.

As he and Colin reached the back wall of the kitchen, the monk turned as if he meant to pace along the building's length. Faucon didn't follow, continuing instead in the direction of the hodgepodge of sheds and barns that stood at the forefront of the household garden.

He shot a laughing glance over his shoulder at the monk. "Where are you going?" he called.

"We aren't walking here?" Colin called back.

"Nay, there's no need for that," Faucon returned.

Colin lifted the hem of his habit and trotted after his Crowner, scattering the few ducks and chickens that yet lingered hopefully near the back of the kitchen. "Why not?"

"Because Mistress Nanette was at the table when Mistress Alina went down to the workroom for the second time. She stayed there until her mistress returned."

"And why does that matter?" Colin pried.

Faucon grimaced. He didn't much like the thought of putting all his eggs into a basket filled with nothing but a few scraps of linen, but that was all he had in hand just now. Yet again, the bits and pieces he'd gathered thus far rearranged themselves but there was still so much missing, nothing came of it. And those bits he craved would remain missing until he could speak with Peter or find a way to compel Hodge to share honestly with him.

"I'm not sure, save that it does," he finally said with a shake of his head.

Together they passed the final shed, where the hogs who'd been granted another day of life were burrowing into the straw for their nightly rest. Near their pen stood a bank of beehives, their homes small domed baskets woven from willow withes, the hives giving off a gentle hum.

As they reached the garden, Faucon squinted, both his nose and eyes burning. These long rows had just received a fresh layer of manure. That said the household had already harvested the last of their turnips and beets, packed their cabbages into their dairy or ice house and shucked their dried beans into baskets for winter storage. All that remained of this growing season, now that Martinmas would soon be at hand, was to plant the over-wintering garlic and cold-weather beans.

Although the garden was a goodly swath of land, perhaps thrice that which belonged to a croft supporting a villager and his family, it wasn't land enough to provide Bernart's household with all its needs. No doubt like many other merchants, he either purchased what he required from the city's grossiers, or his household owned fields outside the town walls that provided the grain for their daily bread.

A line of carefully-pruned apple trees stood at the back of the garden. Here and there, yellowed leaves yet clung to their otherwise barren and gnarled branches. Hanging low and heavy above their foreshortened crowns was a cloud of smoke.

"What burns?" Colin asked, but Faucon had already picked up his heels to jog in the direction of the fire.

It wasn't until he'd ducked under the low-hanging branches of the first tree that he saw Gisla. Dressed only in her yellow undergown, Bernart's daughter sat on a backless wooden bench. Shoulders hunched and arms crossed over her chest, she stared into the pit. Tears trickled unheeded down her face.

"Mistress Gisla," Colin said as he joined Faucon, naught but comfort in his tone.

She gasped in surprise, wiping her face with the backs of her hands even before she looked to see who came. As she recognized them, she once more donned that arrogance of hers, throwing it over her shoulders like a cloak. "Brother Colin, what do you here?" she asked in the same cold, commanding tone she'd taken with Faucon.

"I was with Master Gerard when Sir Crowner's clerk came begging witnesses to swear to your father's ancestry," the monk said, as if he were accustomed to women speaking so rudely to him.

He went to the bench, then sat close beside her. "Ach, lass. I'm so sorry this happened to you," he said gently, extending an arm in the offer of an embrace. Unlike Edmund, Colin apparently paid no heed to his order's ban on physical contact with women.

Much to Faucon's amazement, Gisla melted into the monk's arm, lowered her head to his breast and began to sob. Colin closed his other arm around her and rocked her gently as she wept.

Leaving the monk to comfort the girl as best he could, Faucon moved to the edge of the pit, and confirmed for himself that this was the place where the household burned what it couldn't remake, reuse or sell off. Gisla's dark blue overgown with its myriad of precious golden stars smoldered atop the ashes. Choked by the cloth, the fire but smoked fitfully, craving that next breath of air that would stir it to a blaze.

He picked up a stick and pushed at the garment. Beneath it lay the charred remains of yet more fabric. He poked and prodded until he found an untouched piece of that second garment. It was about the length of his arm and smut-stained, but he could see that it had started the day a pretty rose color sewn with swirling dark green threads to look like ivy. This must have been the gown Alina had worn until she'd befouled it with her husband's blood this afternoon. He dug deeper into the thick layer of ashes. There was nothing—no gowns or, more importantly, footwear—to be found.

On the bench, Gisla's sobs were ebbing into sad hiccoughs. Faucon sent Colin a warning look. Shadows were closing in. It wouldn't be much longer before they'd have to leave this place or be caught in darkness. The monk nodded.

"Come lass, breathe deep," he told the proud girl. "I know your sire is gone, but you needn't lose Peter as well, of this I am certain. Sir Crowner has questions for you. The sooner you answer him, the more swiftly he can prove it wasn't your sweetheart who did this awful thing."

Gisla gave a quiet cry at that. Pushing back from the monk, she wiped her face with her sleeves, then swiveled on the bench to look up at Faucon. "How can you do that?" she pleaded, sounding and looking like nothing more than a bereft and lovelorn girl. "That's the inquest jury in our yard."

"And they have only sworn to confirm my verdict that your father was murdered. I didn't name Peter as his murderer," Faucon told her. "Mistress, help me by answering my questions in all honesty, knowing I will do what I can to prove what I know in my heart, that

Peter didn't kill your sire. Be warned, though. This isn't a vow. I cannot know how to resolve your sire's murder until I speak with Peter and hear what he saw, and I may not be able to do that for another forty days."

Gisla drew another bracing breath and gave a last shudder as she reclaimed her cloak of authority—the one her father had woven for her from the silver that filled his chests. It was a garment she wore more easily than did her mother. "If speaking to Peter is what you need, I will see that you do. Indeed, I'll see that it happens on the morrow if it is your desire."

Faucon smiled in understanding. The church was adding a tower, with all the costs that went with such an addition. Silver would make its way from one chest into another, and doors would open. "That would suit very well," he replied with a grateful nod.

"So, describe for me the details of this day, especially the meal and your father's absence from it," he continued. "Did anything out of the ordinary occur in the hours prior to your father's passing?"

Gisla again wrapped her arms around herself and turned her gaze toward the pit. It no longer smoldered. Stirred to it by Faucon's prodding, the flames had found what they craved. Hungry tongues filled with warmth and light crackled in joy, sending up dancing sparks, as they cheerfully consumed the blood-stained fabric.

"I think this day was no different than any other," the girl said, watching her gown curl and brown, "save that we were to have slaughtered Gog and Magog, the last of our hogs," she said.

Faucon eyed her, in surprise. He didn't know anyone who named their hogs. The choice of their names was even stranger. His nurse had more than once told him the tale of the ancient giant Gogmagog.

"Mama meant to do the deed right after the meal so their carcasses could hang the night in the cold air,"

Gisla was saying.

Her phrasing made Faucon frown. "You cannot mean that your mother meant to slaughter them herself?"

Gisla nodded, again staring into the flames, then corrected herself. "Well, Mama doesn't do the skinning or the gutting. She just cannot bear that anyone else might deal them their death blows, fearing they might be caused unnecessary pain. That's because she always becomes too fond of our piggies, making them into pets. But she never had the chance to do the task because of what happened to Papa."

Another shuddering sigh left her. "As for our meal, it too, was like any other. At least of late."

Opening her crossed arms, she clenched her fists as they lay in her lap. "Would that Papa had not made me his confidante and that he'd never taken that last journey to London," she said harshly. "He's been horrible since he returned. That mercer he met there is an incubus, who filled my father's ears with the promise of the incredible wealth and riches possible were he to move our trade to London town."

"This is the man to whom your father offered you in marriage?" Faucon asked. He wondered if it was the mark of a woman's trade that a man might share such intimate information with a daughter, who otherwise had no right to such knowledge.

"You know of that?" The girl cried in surprise.

Faucon nodded. "Your mother mentioned there was a recent contract offered for your hand," he told her.

She gave a sharp shake of her head. "Nay, the mercer isn't that man. Papa intended me for some London goldsmith whom this godforsaken mercer knew. Nay, that black-hearted silk merchant dangled his own daughter before Papa, telling my father that he could shuck my mother because she has given him no heir save me."

Faucon gaped. Colin stared wide-eyed at the girl. "But the trade is your mother's," the monk protested. "Bernart would own nothing if he set aside your mother."

Gisla shook her head. "That might have been true for my grandmother when my grandfather gave over his business in favor of hers. But since Papa and Mama have been married, our trade has become firmly established in his name, even if what we produce yet rests upon Mama's shoulders. Mistress Nanette has seen to it our journeywomen and apprentices are every bit as skilled as either Mama or I. That makes both of us no more than one needle among many others, something that my mother encouraged," she added, a note of disapproval in her voice.

"I fear she's not the tradeswoman my grandmother was," she finished, glancing from Crowner to monk, then back to Faucon.

"Should my father have freed himself of Mama, then married me into a different trade, he could have simply continued doing what he always had, claiming mastery while Nanette and the others provided the skill. And if he were to have moved the trade to London, there'd be none to know what might have come before or the terrible trick he'd pulled upon my mother.

"Or on me, I suppose, since I would have inherited after Mama," she added, then shook her head. "But I cannot believe he intended me hurt. From the way Papa spoke of this goldsmith, I know he believed he was giving me a life far grander than even this one," she waved a hand in the direction of her fine home. "It was the sort of life he wanted for himself, not one I craved," she added at a whisper.

She paused, the firelight showing the hard hurt lines of her face. "Such was the filth this mercer poured into my sire's ears. When Papa first confided all this to me,

I did what I could to reason with him, pleading on Mama's behalf. When that failed, I tried telling him how annulling their marriage would make me a bastard and lower my value to this goldsmith. He said there was no need for an annulment, not when time had proven my mother barren."

Colin shook his head at that. "I cannot believe your father could ever have swayed anyone in our holy Church that he needed a son to carry on his trade. Not only is your trade not his, it's a woman's trade, and you are a woman. Thus he has the heir he needs to carry his business into the next generation."

Faucon cocked a brow at this. "My pardon if I insult, Brother Colin, but Master Bernart had the wealth he needed to sway the opinions of such men, no matter how holy."

The monk offered a wry smile at this. "No insult taken, Sir Crowner. Aye, Bernart had the coins, but any abbot or bishop who studied his plea would be hard-pressed to see their way clear to make use of that silver without raising complaints from their superiors."

Colin looked at Gisla. "This is especially so when it's clear that your mother isn't barren, or rather she wasn't barren when she bore your father his three children. And he has his heir. That fact is incontrovertible and, I believe, insurmountable in such an argument."

Shivering, Gisla fell silent at that. Staring into the pit, she watched as the last of her fine gown, and the family which had provided it for her, went up in smoke. As the fabric was consumed, the flames began to die back, taking with them both heat and light as they expired.

Faucon released the pin that held his mantle over his shoulders, fastening it to his tunic before he offered her his garment. She gave him a swift smile, the movement of her mouth that of a wary child grateful for an unexpected kindness. He nodded in return, understanding better what it was she hid beneath her rudeness.

"So, did your father tell your mother of his intention?" he asked, certain that Bernart had done so.

To his surprise, Gisla shook her head. "Nay, Papa said he told no one save me, and me he swore to secrecy, trusting that my love for him would insure his privacy. I gave him my word only because, just like you, Brother Colin," she said, looking at the monk, "I couldn't see how he'd ever gain what he intended. Indeed, as days passed, I saw I was right. Papa went back and forth to the abbey, but it seemed no amount of treasure he offered was enough to purchase the answer he craved. That's when he began avoiding our table each and every day rather than occasionally, doing so to spite my mother.

"Whipped to it by that evil mercer, his greed had grown so all-consuming that he couldn't admit his plan was mad. Or, futile. Instead, he blamed Mama for standing between him and the wealth he was now convinced should belong to him alone."

Again Gisla sighed. "So, up and down my mother went at every meal, growing ever more ashamed that her husband would make such a show of his disregard for her. Today was no different."

Just then, the church bells began to toll, each to its own rhythm and on its own note. The hour of Vespers had arrived. With it the town gates would close, and the citizens of Stanrudde would rest easy in the safety of their walls for the night.

"Mistress," Faucon said, casting a glance at the darkening sky, "it's time we returned you to the house."

"If I must," she muttered resentfully, but came to her feet like the dutiful, loving daughter she was.

"Tell me what happened after your mother found your father dead, after she raised the hue and cry," Faucon said, as the three of them made their way through the trees and into the garden. "What did you and she do in the workshop after you came down at her call?"

She was quiet for a moment as she gathered her thoughts. "When Mama began shrieking, all the household leapt up from the table to run to her," she said, watching her feet as she spoke. "I was the last to reach the workshop. I sit at the upper table, the one farthest from the door. By the time I was coming down the stairs, Mama was screaming that Papa was dead and Peter had killed him."

Dragging Faucon's mantle closer around her, she pulled its collar up around her chin as if she wanted to disappear into its depths. "I didn't want to see," she whispered. "I just wanted everything to go back to the way it had been, before all this."

"You didn't want to see, but you entered anyway, did you not? So what met your gaze as you entered?" Colin prodded gently.

She kept her attention on her hem. "There was blood," she shuddered. "Papa lay in it. It was all over Mama's hands and gowns, and on Nanette."

"Mistress Nanette was in the workshop with your mother?" Faucon interrupted.

"Aye. Nanette had just then climbed the stair on her return from the kitchen when Mama left the table that final time. She followed Mama to the workshop door, or so she told me later as she and I undressed Mama, and I helped Nanette into clean garments. You arrived before I had the chance to change my own gowns," Gisla told Faucon, then continued.

"Nanette told me that she'd followed Mama down the stairs, but waited outside the workshop, thinking she gave my parents their privacy. She said an instant later Peter raced past her to escape out our door as Mama began shouting of murder. Indeed, Mama flew after him as if she meant to chase him down herself.

Nanette said she followed Mama into the yard and caught her to keep her from doing so, but Mama must have insisted on returning to the workshop, for that's where I saw them. Mama was on her knees beside Papa, sobbing and pressing her hands to his throat as if to close his wound while Nanette was trying to drag Mama back from him."

Gisla paused, taking a few steps before continuing. "Or mayhap Mama was standing over Papa while it was Nanette leaning over Papa seeking signs of life." She shook her head. "Nay, it cannot have been that way. Mama wore Papa's blood all over her gowns and hands. She'd even smeared what stained her onto Nanette and, shortly after that, onto my outer gown."

At last, she sighed. "My pardon. Would that I could be more precise, but this day is such a jumble in my thoughts. I just know that I best like the idea of Mama trying to save Papa's life, even if he was already gone and despite all the wrong he'd planned to do her."

Colin put his arm around the girl's back. "Tell me if you can. Was your father's wound still oozing blood when you saw him?"

Gisla made a gagging sound and stopped. Faucon and the monk stood with her. "I don't know," she cried, her voice high and reedy. "I am such a coward. I should have been the one trying to close his wound as my mother had done. All I'm sure of is that this whole day feels like a horrible dream."

They stayed where they stood, waiting for her to collect herself. Overhead, bats had replaced the birds in the sky, the flying mice darting and dashing. In the stillness of the gathering gloom, Faucon could hear the sounds of the jury, men chatting to each other in low voices as they made their shuffling way around Bernart's body, Edmund's voice as he asked their names.

So too, had the sounds of city life changed as night

came on. The clanging of hammers in the smithies was no more. That persistent noise had been replaced by a discordant cacophony of music. Here, a sackbut, there a pipe and tambour, nearer still a viol, each one playing a different tune. Instead of shop owners calling out about the quality of their wares, those men and women who liked darkness better than light bellowed in laughter or shared bawdy songs.

"Can you tell us what you did after you entered the workroom?" Faucon asked gently as Gisla started forward again, leading them through the dim shadows clinging to the sheds and outbuildings as they made their way into the courtyard.

That teased a choked laugh from her. "I went to my father's side as my mother had done, thinking to kiss his brow in farewell. But as I leaned forward, my fingers found the pool of blood on the floor. I stained my hands and the sleeves on both my gowns."

She held up her arms for them to see. Her undergown had fitted sleeves, laced tightly at her wrists. Even in the dark, Faucon could see that their lower edges were discolored.

"I couldn't help myself after that. I fled, following my mother and Nanette up the stairs to help settle Mama. I suppose it's just as well I did. It took both Nanette and me to strip those bloody gowns from her," she finished at a sigh. "They were ruined. That's why I burnt them."

They stopped in front of her home's grand doorway. Faucon pushed open the heavy wooden panel, then stepped aside so she might enter ahead of him. As she stepped around it, she gave a quiet cry and stopped.

Both he and Colin shifted to see past the door. Faint light flickered out of the open workshop door. Colin crossed himself. Faucon wondered if he did so against the possibility that this was the light of Bernart's soul, yet trapped in the earthly realm.

"Who is there?" Gisla demanded.

As she strode for the workshop door, reclaiming her role as the mistress Faucon had met only two hours ago, he and Colin followed. It was the lasses, returned to the workroom with their cloths and soap, although they cleaned by the uncertain light of a single tallow lamp. They were plying their rags more vigorously this time, now that Bernart's congealed blood had been removed. Still, the younger of the two was crying softly as she worked.

Faucon looked at the far end of the worktable. That troublesome counting board still sat there. The lamp was bright enough to show him that the coins were also still in place.

"What are you two doing in here at this hour?" their mistress asked of the lasses.

"Mistress Nanette says we must finish scrubbing the chamber floor this night," replied the elder girl with a shaking voice, "so no one will see it befouled upon the morrow."

"Mistress Nanette is wrong," Gisla said, yet clinging to the workshop doorway. "No one will see this chamber on the morrow because the door will be closed and locked. Go now. If she chides, tell her I said as much."

Just as they had done once before, the two fled the room as swiftly as possible, taking their tools but leaving behind their lamp. After moving aside to let them pass, Gisla retreated to stand in the doorway. Her gaze was locked on the floor where her father had bled his last.

"Mistress, help me with something," Faucon said, entering the chamber, leaving her and Colin to stop in front of the blood-stained board. "This suggests your father was paying wages when he was struck down."

She nodded, yet struggling to free her gaze from the place where her father ended his life. "Aye, he would have been. Today was the day for it." Her voice was flat and quiet.

"Then where are his tally sticks?" Faucon asked.

That caught her attention. Blinking, she aimed her gaze at the worktable and the counting board. "What is this?" she cried.

As Colin stayed where he stood, she picked up the lamp—naught but a clay bowl in which melting fat fed burning wick—then joined him. "Where are they?" she asked, speaking to herself as she eyed the board.

Bending over, she reached deep under the table. There was the dull clink of metal against metal, then she brought out an iron ring on which hung as many keys as there were strongboxes in this chamber. Going to a central chest, she opened the lock that closed the iron band encircling it. The chest's hinges creaked a little as she lifted the lid.

Holding the lid high with one hand, she raised her lamp until it illuminated the interior of the box. "Thank the Lord, they're here," she breathed in relief, then gave a quiet shriek and stumbled back a step, letting the lid slam shut.

Needing to see what upset her, Faucon lifted the lid for himself. Inside, a shallow tray hung from braces fastened to the sides of the box. The tray completely filled the space, obscuring whatever lay in the belly of the chest. In that tray were several dozen wooden wands, each of these tally sticks a little longer than his hand. Carved into the top of each stick was the unique mark that named the account holder. There were flowers, stars, curling lines, fish and more. Slashed along their lengths were any number of evenly spaced cuts. Some wore but a few of these notches while others bore cuts from top to bottom. Even by the light of a single lamp, he could see the dark streaks and spots of blood that stained them.

"Who put those in there?" Gisla demanded shakily

from where she stood. The trembling of her hand made light dance wildly across the walls around them.

Faucon offered her a quick glance, then looked back at the tray. "The one who arranged your sire's death." But not the one who had caused his death. "Would your father have left those keys of yours upon the table while he worked?"

"He might have," Gisla said with considering frown. "Papa wasn't concerned about his things in here because he had no need for caution, not in here. We can bar the workshop door while we work. Nor is it a great secret about where we keep the ring, mostly because we can also lock the workshop door from the outside, thus protecting what we keep within this chamber."

That was disappointing. "I still don't understand why the tally sticks were put away when the coins were left out where anyone could take them," he said.

Gisla pivoted to look at the board and gave another quiet cry, this one less of fright than surprise. Setting the lamp on the table, she gathered up her skirt with one hand to form a sack, then lifted the other, preparing to sweep the coins off the board and into the fabric of her skirt.

"Wait!" Faucon cried out. "First, tell me if what you see here looks usual for the wages you pay."

Still holding her skirt as a sack with one hand, she shifted to stand directly in front of the board. With her index finger, she tapped each of the squares that held coins, then pushed at the tumbled pennies. Her lips moved soundlessly as she counted.

"Aye, this amount is our usual. Papa must have just finished his task when"—she drew a deep breath—"it happened."

Then she scraped the coins off the board into her makeshift sack. Turning, she dumped the bloodied bits of silver into the tally stick tray. This she did when

Faucon was certain that hidden beneath the drawer was a purse short by the number of coins upon the board.

Locking the chest, Gisla returned the keys to the hidden peg under the table. This she did with her head turned to the side, so she needn't look at dark stain that marked the spot where her father died. As she retreated toward the doorway, she removed Faucon's mantle from her shoulders. She held it out to him as he joined her near the door, offering him a small but grateful smile.

"Mistress, before I leave you, I have one more thing to ask," he said as he donned his outer garment. "I fear it's of a private nature."

Taking that as his cue, Colin shifted into the room, pulling the door closed behind him. The chamber dropped into dimness, what with only that spit of friendly orange light from the tallow lamp and the little torchlight from the courtyard that managed to spill in through the open windows.

"Ask what you will," she told him, nodding her permission for him to speak as he would. "I'll answer if I can."

Faucon cleared his throat. "I have been told that you and Peter are trysting," he said, releasing what he knew would be a bolt right into her already aching heart, destroying what was left of her pride.

Giving a quiet cry, she buried her face into her palms. "How can you know that?" she begged, stumbling back to lean against the nearest chest as she peered at him through her fingers.

"Your mother and Mistress Nanette said as much to me," Faucon said gently.

"Nay!" Gisla gasped out, spreading her fingers to peer at him through them. "I never said...they never...how can they know?" She bent her head and her shoulders shook.

"Sweetling," Colin said, crossing to lean against the

chest next to her, once more wrapping an arm around her shoulders, "such things are never as hidden as you think. People see. Even if it's just a glimpse, they still talk, even if what they say isn't the whole truth."

Faucon spoke over him. "It's vital that you tell me where the two of you met and if you did so at a regular time. Most importantly, I need to know how you arranged these meetings with Peter."

She dropped her hands. This time, she made no attempt to scrub away her emotions when she looked up at him. Her lips trembled.

"You'll not believe me, I know, but I vow to you that Peter and I have never done anything untoward. We met only to enjoy each other's company," she said, her voice soft, her words broken. "We began doing so after my sire returned from London, full of greed and plans. I—I never meant to dishonor my parents, but how could I even consider marrying another when for the past five years I've believed that Peter would be my husband?" she protested, defending herself.

Faucon smiled at that. "Take heart. If Peter can be proven innocent, I think Master Roger will swiftly see the two of you wed, paying no heed to whatever more recent agreements your father might have made."

"Thank you," Gisla offered quietly, her honest gratitude rising from the depths of her soul.

"So how did you arrange your meetings?" Faucon asked again.

"It was against the timing of Peter's schedule. On those days when he left fabric with Master Hodge for bleaching, his route home brought him by our house around the time that our midday meal ended. That hour, the one just after we've left the table, is the busiest of the day. The servants are intent on completing their tasks before nightfall, while Nanette's women are settling back into their own work, taking advantage of the day's brightest hours. That was also the hour Papa would lock himself into the workroom, doing so for the same reason, because of the light. As for my mother, she likes to nap for an hour after eating.

"I thought they were all too busy to notice," she added at a shamed whisper, then sighed. "Most often, Peter came to me in the garden, behind the apple trees. He'd climb Master Gerard's wall, then steal across their garden to ours. I truly never thought anyone would see us there."

"Most often? Then there is a second place for your meetings?" Faucon asked, utterly certain what her answer would be but wanting to hear her speak the words.

Even with the light so low, Faucon saw shame burn on her face. "Aye," she said quietly. "From time to time, my father delivers our projects himself, if the destination isn't so far. It's something he's done a half-dozen times in the last few months. While he's away, I take on all his tasks, including counting out coins for purchases and wages." Her voice trailed off into silence.

Faucon nodded. "As I thought. You came in here, barred the door, then opened the far window for Peter to crawl through, aye?"

The far window was close enough to the courtyard wall that a determined man could move from wall top to window and slither through the open into the workshop. There was little chance he'd be seen doing so, not with the men in the storehouse, standing with their heads bowed over fabric and their backs to the yard. There was also little chance that such a man would detour to the storehouse to retrieve a pair of scissors to use as a weapon.

"Aye, that is what I have done," she admitted, then continued more boldly, "but not what I did today. My father had no delivery so I never sent for Peter. I don't know why he came today." She shook her head in true confusion.

"By what means did you tell Peter when and where to come?" Colin asked, patting her hand.

She glanced between the two men, her love for Peter at war with her shame. "Each morning, he walks past our house. There's a broken stone in the wall near our front gate. I made two ribbons, both embroidered with flax flowers."

Here she sighed, then her lips lifted into a small sad smile. "Years ago, we promised each other that the flax flower would be the emblem for our house when once we wed. On one ribbon the flower is scarlet. That's the one I would tuck beneath the stone when he was to meet me amongst the apple trees. The other flower is blue. That meant he was to come to the workshop. As for when, I would put pebbles on the ribbon. One pebble was one hour after None, two for two hours."

"So this morn, if your love had seen the ribbon that had the blue flower upon it and no pebble, he would have believed you wanted him to come to the workshop around the hour of None?" Colin again asked.

Gisla's face was a ghostly white within the frame of her fair braids. "Aye, I suppose he could have thought that, but I don't see why he would have. He must know that we can never meet at None because that's the hour for the household's meal. Unlike my sire, I'm never allowed to be absent from the table. Moreover, I left no ribbon for Peter today, so he shouldn't have come at all."

"But he did come," Faucon replied. "He did, because the one who needed him in the workroom at that hour left that sign for him. Where do you keep those ribbons when they aren't in the wall, Mistress?"

The girl gasped and reached for the purse threaded onto her embroidered belt. She thrust her hand into the pouch, only to cry out in dismay as she pulled back empty fingers. "They're gone!"

Faucon stifled his urge to grin in triumph. Peter's

presence in the workroom had indeed been very carefully planned. Of course it had. One of the terms of the union between Gisla and Peter had included Peter becoming master here after Bernart. What better way to negate that contract, such as it was, than to see Gisla's love hanged for her father's murder?

Chapter Twelve

After Colin had bid Mistress Gisla to find her bed, sending her up the stairs with the promise that God and His angels would keep her safe, Faucon and the monk returned to the courtyard. The jurors were gone as was Elsa's body, but Bernart yet lay on the table. In the dimness, the gaping gash across his throat looked blue against the pallor of his cold skin.

Edmund yet sat on his stool, bathed in the oily glow of a flickering torch. He had his arms outstretched before him and was flexing his fingers as if to ease their aching.

"Sir Faucon," he called when he saw his master, "you are just in time. The inquest is complete and all is recorded as it must be. A good day's work done and done efficiently, if I do say so myself," he added in satisfaction.

"Then so you should say, Brother Edmund," Faucon called back as he and Colin started toward him.

"Sir Crowner, your patterns," Tom said, stepping out of the open doorway of the now-darkened storehouse. He held out the bits of linen Rob had cut. "I'm glad I found you. Once we take our master back within the house, the door will close and we'll not be out again until the morrow."

Faucon took the thin sheets of fabric, folding them until he could tuck them into the purse that hung from his belt with his gloves. "My thanks again to you and your brother."

Tom's reply was a single nod. "I hope you find the

one who wears that shoe, sir. Our master may not have been the best of men, but no one deserves to die thusly in his own home."

Then, turning toward the open door behind him, he called, "Come all of you. It's time to fetch the master inside so he might be washed and wrapped."

Two men came with Rob to join Tom. The four of them hurried ahead of Faucon and Colin to lift Bernart's unresponsive weight between them. Then, grunting, they bore their former master on their shoulders as they returned him to his fine house for one last time.

As they departed, Faucon smiled at his clerk. "Brother Edmund, I cannot speak for you, but I know my belly reminds me of how little I've eaten this day. Brother Colin and I are meeting an acquaintance of mine at an alewife's shop. Will you join us?" Just as Bernart put food upon his table for those he employed, it was Faucon's duty to supply Edmund's meals.

"Nay, I'm for the abbey," his clerk replied, then aimed a hard look at his fellow monk. "It's a fast day today, Brother. I think you should return with me to the abbey as well rather than courting temptation by lingering where men make a show of savoring food and drink."

It was no request. While Faucon bit his tongue to keep himself from chiding his small-minded clerk, something Colin wouldn't allow him to do, Colin bowed his head. In that instant, his demeanor shifted from the intelligent friend Faucon appreciated to the humble lay brother Edmund expected.

"Indeed, it is a day of fasting, Brother Edmund, and so I have done all the day long," the commoner said. "Please harbor no concerns on my behalf, secure in the knowledge that Abbot Athelard does not. I but go with Sir Crowner to show him this place, he being a newcomer to our town. Once he's there, I'll return to the abbey."

Colin paused to look at Faucon. "Tell me, Sir Crowner, now that you are locked within our city walls for the night. Have you accommodations?"

"Not as of yet," Faucon replied. "I'll admit I hoped Abbot Athelard might offer me your guest house."

"I fear that isn't possible, not tonight," Colin replied with a shake of his head. "Our abbot holds aside that space, expecting the arrival of a bishop's private secretary who comes either late this night or on the morrow. I cannot promise you that the alewife will have space for you, but should you find nothing else, there is a comfortable corner in my stillroom. It's not much, but it would suit a man who isn't overly fastidious about where he lays his head."

Faucon caught back his laugh. Just as Colin knew his way around a corpse, so too did the monk understand how to circumvent Edmund's unbending attitude.

"That would be a gift, indeed. I'm sure your stillroom will be quieter and cleaner than an alewife's house," he replied. "Would you mind remaining with me for the duration? The man I'm meeting isn't one to chat, so I doubt I'll linger long at the alewife's house. It would be a welcome boon if you were to stay to lead me to your stillroom when the time comes. Perhaps Brother Edmund will be comforted with my promise to see you aren't tempted to break your fast."

"That I can do, Sir Crowner. With Brother Edmund's permission, of course," Colin said, his head still bowed.

"Go then with Sir Faucon, Brother," Edmund said, "knowing that I will be looking for you at Compline service tonight. Sir Faucon, if it's no trouble to you, I'd like to attend morning prayers with my brothers before we leave Stanrudde on the morrow," Edmund continued as he slid off Bernart's stool. He picked up his traveling basket and prepared to pack his tools. "Perhaps we might stay our departure until after Terce?"

Faucon grimaced at the thought of leaving Stanrudde without resolving the matter of Bernart's death. But there was nothing more he could do with what little he had at the moment. Nor had he any hope that he might have gathered anything more before mid-morning on the morrow. Somehow he doubted that the shoemakers would put aside paying business to sort through who knew how many patterns on the behalf of a man they didn't know. Nay, if the shoemakers were willing to find that pattern for him, it would happen in their leisure hours. He feared Peter would have to linger a good while longer in his wrongful prison, even if the webber managed to confirm what Faucon now suspected.

"After Terce it will be, then," he said to Edmund, nodding his agreement. Well, at least that gave him until almost midday to distribute his patterns, doing so without his clerk's interference. "On the morrow, then."

Leaving Edmund to make his own way to the abbey, Faucon and Colin started out Bernart's gate, once more following the path of Peter's flight, this time moving in the proper direction. As they walked, Colin entertained his Crowner by pointing out this shop and that home, offering tales of the lives that had been lived in them.

It was on their second turn that Faucon sensed those who followed. He shot a quick glance over his shoulder. There were five. Unlike the groups who sang their drunken way down the lanes, laughing and shouting insults to one another, or those who strutted along, seeking trouble or a whore, these men came on with purpose and moving as one. It was the precision of their movement that named them soldiers, and in that precision Faucon identified the one who'd sent them.

His mouth set in a grim line. However inconvenient, their appearance in Stanrudde at this particular moment wasn't unexpected. He'd seen their master today on the road after he'd departed from Blacklea. All that remained was to determine who would play the fox and who the hare in this encounter.

Keeping his head bent in the posture of a listener, Faucon again released the pin that held his mantle close around him, fastening that pretty bit of metal to his tunic. With no buckler for his left hand, the possibility of wrapping his mantle around his arm was the best he could do. That was, if he could manage to turn his garment around his hand without tripping over it or otherwise hampering his own defense.

Pulling his shoulders forward to keep his outer garment balanced on them, he claimed his gloves from where they'd spent the day tucked into his belt. He donned them beneath the shield of his mantle, then repositioned and loosened his sword.

Colin led them around the next corner and into a narrow alley. The inviting aroma Faucon had noted earlier was muted now, no doubt much of the alewife's wares having been consumed in the past hour. With nightfall, her daytime trade wisely departed for their homes, finding safety behind their own barred doors, as should all good folk do. That left her her nighttime trade, those from whom good folk should always flee, free to creep out of hiding, ready to seek out what perverted pleasures they could under the cloak of darkness.

Faucon eyed the alleyway. This was the perfect place for the assault he expected. Not only were there no windows overlooking the alley in any of the houses that lined it, he suspected those who lived here knew better than to involve themselves in a stranger's misfortune. Moreover, those who followed him would come for him here as they no more wanted to be seen than Faucon wished others to see them.

Colin laughed at something he'd just said, something Faucon hadn't heard.

"Brother," he said softly, "I need you to do me a boon, one that may well save my life. I'll be needing the man you call Richard Alwynason at my side in a moment or two."

Even in the dark, he could see the monk's eyes fly wide at his request. Colin's mouth opened. Faucon carefully shook his head in warning. God bless the man, he understood, and neither looked behind them nor blurted questions.

"What do we do now?" Colin whispered, bowing his head as he crossed his arms, tucking his hands into his sleeves.

"*We* do nothing. All the help I need is in the man you'll warn, begging him as you do to come to me in silence," he replied. "After that, you'll stay inside the alewife's door until he or I call for you. For the now, we walk until those behind us force the issue."

Then, raising his voice to its normal tone, Faucon said, "So, tell me about this alewife and her wares. Not that I need you to speak words when my nose tells me I'll enjoy this meal."

Again, Colin followed where he led without hesitation, starting in on the alewife's tale. The five steadily closed the gap between them for another half a perch. A sharp whistle pierced the air.

"Now, Brother," Faucon said calmly.

As Colin sprinted down the alley, Faucon turned, swinging his mantle out over his head with his left hand. Although only fabric and fur, his unexpected movement was enough to confuse his attackers for an instant. That was hesitation enough for Faucon to draw his sword and get his mantle wound twice around his left hand.

Then they were on him. Holding his wrapped arm

before him as a shield, he caught the first one's shorter sword on his own. With a shriek of metal, he twisted his weapon free, then smashed its hilt into this one's face. As the man's nose and cheekbone broke, he screamed and fell to the side, colliding with two of his mates.

Steel nipped at the flesh of his left shoulder. Faucon danced to the side, tempting his attacker to follow. The fool did. Faucon's foot met the man's knee with enough force to knock his leg out from beneath him. As this one toppled, he shifted, sword flashing as he drove its tip into the next man's throat. His assailant dropped, well on his way to death.

Yanking his sword clear, Faucon danced back. There were four yet afoot, but the man he'd stunned swayed helplessly behind his companions, his face darkened with blood.

Two came at once. He pivoted, slamming his shoulder into one as he caught the other's blade with his gloved hand and twisted. The man's sword flew. From the corner of his eye he saw the third man swing his weapon toward his unprotected neck.

Faucon bent his knees and swiveled. The blow glanced off his upper back, cutting into flesh and cloth and sending him staggering. One knee barely touched the earth before he was rising and turning. As he did, one of his attackers dropped before him, blood gushing from his throat the way it had from Bernart earlier this day. The warm wet spray spattered Faucon's face.

Another piercing whistle tore through unnatural quiet in the alley. In an instant the three who could yet walk were gone, leaving behind their dead or dying companions.

Panting in exertion, Faucon leaned against the wall behind him and shrugged his shoulders. They both moved without pain, telling him that nothing of import was injured, although he would surely ache on the morrow. Still, blood trickled down his back, sticky and warm, staining another man's garment. He made a face, guessing it would take needle and thread to repair both him and Sir John's tunic.

As Temric FitzHenry, or Richard Alwynason, crouched to wipe his knife blade on the fallen man's tunic, the older warrior looked up at Faucon. "I was told to make no sound as I came," he said, his tone amused. "May I assume it's safe to speak now?"

"Aye, you may, but I think I'll speak first," Faucon said with a grateful smile as his rescuer came to his feet. "By God, I'm glad you agreed to meet with me this night. If the day comes when you have such a need, know that I am yours."

The knight who was not a knight almost smiled at that. "For the sake of my half-brothers who love you, glad I am I was here to assist. Although I think the news you crave of them should wait for another meeting. Brother Colin was none too happy at being commanded to stay away. Once he's got you, I expect he'll busy himself tending to your needs."

Then the knight toed the man whose throat he'd cut. "Tell me, Sir Crowner. Shall we raise the hue and cry, and chase down these evildoers?"

"As this shire's Crowner I pronounce their killings justified," Faucon replied with a breath of a laugh, then he sighed. "I would just as well throw these two into the nearest cesspit. I'd rather they weren't identified."

"How so?" Temric asked.

An explanation was the least he owed this soldier. "The one who sent these dogs did so believing that the outcome would be in his favor no matter how this encounter ended. If I died, he would be rid of me and all I represent to him. He would then be free to replace me with a man of his own choosing. But he was equally prepared for me to live on past this attack. Now that I have, he'll expect me to come for him, making accusations of attempted murder. He'll meet my accusations with cries of besmirched honor, then challenge me when I'm not yet ready to meet him sword to sword. But, if his men are identified, I'll have no choice in the matter. If I don't make the expected charges, I'll seem a coward."

"Ah," the older man replied in understanding, "thus costing you the respect of every man in the shire."

Faucon nodded. To lose the respect of those in this shire so soon in the term of his appointment meant he'd never command the authority he needed to do what was expected of him. And if he failed at his tasks, he'd not only disappoint his great-uncle, he'd lose his twenty pounds a year.

"As you can see, this man believed no matter what happened, he would be rid of me," Faucon repeated. "The only factor he hadn't considered when he sent his men to follow me to Stanrudde was that there might be someone here who could come to my aid."

As the words left Faucon's mouth, the bits and pieces he held so precious shuffled, moving until the tale they told began to unfold. He grinned, at last understanding why the coins had been left on the board. Aye, who, indeed, was the fox and who the hare?

The older knight freed a harsh breath. "Well, as far as these two, I think you're in luck. It just so happens there are a few men inside the alehouse I suspect know how to make such offal disappear. I'll pay them on your behalf, guarding your anonymity, and happily take in trade your promise of future aid. Although it's a poor trade on my part, I think. I cannot imagine ever needing such assistance now that I have given up the warrior's life to become a city man. Good night to you, Sir Faucon. I'll send Brother Colin to you."

Much to Faucon's surprise, this usually humorless man offered him a smile. As Temric's mouth lifted, the shadows rearranged themselves, flowing over the rough lines of his face, highlighting the rise of his cheekbones and bend of his nose. His eyes were but a bare gleam.

"At the moment, I find myself thinking it may be a good thing to know a Crowner, but not such a good thing to be one, at least not in this shire. Rannulf was wise to refuse the position. If my guess is right as to who hunts you, I think you'd be well advised to hire someone to help watch your back."

Then Temric disappeared into the darkness at the back of the alleyway.

Brother Colin's stillroom, where the monk made the concoctions he used in his healing, was hardly more than a shed which stood near the end of the abbey's infirmary. Long and narrow, it had a tile roof and wooden walls. The half dozen tallow lamps the monk had set out so he could see to Faucon's injuries offered more than enough light to show his Crowner every corner of this amazing place.

Only one wall was bare, that being one of the narrow end walls. It had been painted with the image of their Lord healing the leper. A small prie-dieu stood against the painting, no doubt the place where Colin offered up his private prayers in those instances when his work kept him from joining his brothers.

Faucon could see little of the other three walls. Bunches of herbs, each one offering up its fragrance or stink, filled the length of every beam and hung from strings tacked to the tops of the walls. Beneath this leafy ceiling ran line after line of narrow shelving. These shelves were jammed with tiny pots and ewers, stacks of nested bowls and small spoons, mortars with their pestles, and wee wooden boxes, the sort that apothecaries used. Beneath the lowest shelf, the base of the walls was cluttered with sacks of who-knew-what.

A long table took up the center of the chamber. Combs of beeswax as well as pots of goose grease and tallow filled one end. Aligned along its center were three small braziers, a metal bowl sitting atop each one. The only sign of the equipment Colin used for distilling his concoctions was the copper vessel at the far end of the table. Since the still needed fire to do its work, Faucon guessed that the monk did the actual distilling outside the shed.

Stripped to his braies, Faucon sat on a short bench and plied his spoon as he ate the alewife's lamb stew. It was fragrant and tasty, if not very warm. God bless him, Colin had appeared in the alley with a stoppered jug of ale and stew in a small wooden pail, which he'd insisted on carrying for him in deference to his injuries.

Once they'd arrived in the stillroom, Faucon hadn't waited for Colin to find him more than a spoon. What need had he for a bowl when the pail worked well enough? As for the ale, Colin had insisted his Crowner use a cup for that. Faucon had agreed only because that made the rich dark liquid easier to savor. Indeed, he was enjoying it almost as much as the brews made by the alewife in the village of Priors Holden.

"This isn't nearly as deep as I expected," Colin said, as he washed away the last of the blood from the wound on Faucon's back. "It's more scrape than cut. That said, you're missing a goodly patch of skin back here. It'll burn as it heals and leave a strange scar, I fear, although I have an unguent that'll help a bit with that."

The monk had already stitched the cut in his Crowner's upper arm. He'd even applied some wondrous potion to the area that had deadened pain before he'd started sewing. That alone won Faucon's respect and unending gratitude.

"Did I not tell you?" Faucon replied, finishing the last of the stew. "The worst of the whole encounter is that yon tunic isn't mine." He pointed his spoon toward

Sir John's sodden garment, fearing it was ruined now that it was both bloodstained and watermarked. The walk to the abbey had been long enough for the fabric to clot to his wound, and Colin had needed to soak the area before he could remove the tunic. "I cannot return it to the man who owns it both stained and torn."

That made the monk laugh. "In the morning, I'll see to your garment, making sure it's mended and cleaned for you while you make your visit to our shoemakers. I'm sure the abbot can find you a tunic to use on the morrow, that is, if you vow not to allow more brigands to attack you and ruin that one as well."

As he said that, Colin laid a hand on Faucon's right shoulder. "If you are able to visit Peter on the morrow, I think you'd best stay in Herebert's church long enough to offer our Lord a bit of thanks. Both injuries on the left! You won't be away from the tools of your trade for long, if at all. My only concern is how to wrap it, for it will surely seep," he finished, speaking more to himself than Faucon.

Turning to a tall basket that leaned against the far wall, the monk asked, "So, are you going to tell me what happened tonight?"

Faucon laughed, draining his cup, then lifting the jug to squeeze the last drop from it. "After you tell me if Hodge is wed and has any heirs."

Colin pulled a length of linen from the basket, nicked it with a knife then tore it. The fabric whirred softly as it separated, doing so in a straight line. "He's a widower as of half a year ago," he said, as he continued to tear bandages, "although I find it hard to name him so when his was hardly a marriage. Master William arranged the union for Hodge, choosing Maud, the widow of our previous pleykster, so she might train him in her husband's trade. Hodge was an honest lad, and hard working. Yet, despite that he strove mightily, he ever remained the least of William's apprentices. He couldn't understand the value of what Mistress Elinor and her women produced. And because he couldn't, he consistently undersold their products. William was right to find him a more straightforward trade to master.

"As for heirs, nay, Hodge has none. Maud was a toothless crone when they wed, all her own heirs having passed before her. Hodge became more son to her than husband, and he was good to her until she finally left this earthly vale.

"Now, you tell me your tale," the monk demanded, albeit mildly as he brought his strips of linen to the table.

As Faucon's bits and pieces once more shifted, this time falling into what was becoming a pleasing pattern, he smiled and shifted to straddle the end of the bench as Colin indicated. "Tonight's little spat was a message from Sir Alain. He'd prefer that I cease to be a servant of the crown in his shire."

That startled a laugh out of the monk. He shook his finger at Faucon. "Did I not warn you at our first meeting that our lord sheriff wouldn't much like your appointment?"

Faucon grinned. "So you did, and you weren't the only one to offer up words of caution. Lady Marian of Blacklea told me she expected Sir Alain to eat up my bones. Do you think she's right?"

The monk eyed his Crowner for a moment, then gave a slow and negative shake his head. "Although I might have agreed with her two weeks ago, I'm no longer so certain." Then he winked. "Although you do look like death. You're more spattered than Bernart."

Faucon laughed. "Wind your bandages around me, old man, then let me find that corner you promised me."

Chapter Thirteen

Faucon groaned as he awakened. He was indeed sore, but he blamed most of his aching on that new bed of his at Blacklea. It was making him soft. In just two weeks he'd forgotten how to rest easily on an earthen floor with nothing but a straw-stuffed pallet between him and the dirt. Lifting off his mantle, which he'd used as a second blanket, he pushed aside the thin sheet of wool that Colin had offered, then sat up and squinted. The stillroom door stood wide, letting in both dawn's light and morn's chill air.

Although the sun had barely risen—dawn came later now that Winter was almost upon them—the business of the world was already at hand. Small birds darted back and forth across the opening, chittering and commenting happily to each other over the richness of the dying herb garden that spread out before the stillroom door. In the distance, hammers on anvils were already tapping out the beat of the city's heart. Closer to hand, donkeys brayed and sheep bleated. Someone whistled a cheery tune.

Faucon grinned. And he yet lived. He came to his feet, his mantle in hand, then rotated his injured arm and smiled. Not only did he move, he moved well. He shifted his shoulder blade and winced. All things considered, it was a good day. But then, he'd never doubted that Colin knew his trade.

Although the monk was nowhere to be seen, on the corner of the table nearest Faucon was a neatly folded tunic. Blue in color, it was woolen and well made. No doubt it had come from one of the abbey's new novices.

Beside the tunic was a small loaf of bread, a good-sized wedge of cheese and a jug. Pulling the stopper from the jug, Faucon sniffed, then made a face. Not watered wine but watered vinegar.

On the floor beneath all this welcome bounty was a pail of water that was as cold as this morning's air. A cloth hung over the pail's brim. Again Faucon grinned, taking Colin's hint. He didn't bother dressing after he washed, knowing that the monk would want to check his wounds and bandages. Instead, he wrapped his mantle around him and ate, even choking down the vinegar. He was just finishing when Colin returned to his workspace.

"How does Sir Crowner this morn?" the monk asked, throwing back his cowl and disentangling his hands from his wide sleeves. His breath clouded a little as he spoke. "Look here, Dickon. This is Sir Crowner. Sir Crowner, Dickon is my new apprentice."

Only then did Faucon see the oblate tagging along behind the monk. The boy, an extra son or an orphan given over to the convent to be raised by the brothers, could have been no more than eight. A compact child, he had a freckled face and red hair that stood in spikes about his head. In his hands he carried a wad of crumpled linen.

"Good morrow, Dickon," Faucon said in greeting. The lad but smiled shyly at his Crowner. That he was tongue-tied was no doubt the outcome of being raised among the brothers with their mostly silent ways.

"Dickon and I have quite the day ahead of us, so I fear I won't be able to assist you any further as you go about your duties, Sir Crowner," Colin said, sounding disappointed.

"I doubt you'll be missing much, not when I think I'll be on the road for home before midday," Faucon replied with a shake of his head. "However, should something occur, you can rest assured you'll know about it. I'll see to that." Aye, he owed Colin that much.

"My thanks," the monk replied with a nod and a smile. "Now, Dickon and I are here to see to your dressings. If you'll remove your mantle?"

After Faucon set aside his outer garment, Colin plucked at the lengths of linen he'd wrapped about his Crowner's back. They'd loosened overnight, pulled free by Faucon's tossing and turning.

"Dickon, do you see how loose these have become?" the monk said to his red-headed shadow. "They will never stay in place once he dons his tunic. How shall we keep them were they should be?"

The child shook out the fabric he had in his hands, revealing that it was a linen shirt. That was a garment Faucon didn't presently have at hand. His own shirts were yet making their way to Blacklea at a snail-like pace.

Clearing his throat, Dickon glanced between monk and knight. "Aren't we to make him don this? Then you'll pin the bandages to it so they won't shift?"

"Smart lad," Colin complimented with a smile, taking the garment from the boy. "So we shall."

Faucon grinned. Would that the holy brothers with whom he'd begun his education had been as kind or careful with him. If they had been, he might have resisted leaving the Church rather than racing away as fast as he could, eager to take up a warrior's trade.

"Sit and we'll see you properly wrapped again, Sir Crowner," Colin said.

As Faucon did as he was commanded, he looked over his shoulder at the monk and his boy. "Once again, many thanks for your good work, Brother. I move far more easily than I expected to this morn. And thank you as well for providing this clothing. Might I ask where Sir John's tunic has gone?"

"It's already in the hands of our launderers. Although I think I should warn you," Colin replied as he worked. "They're not certain they can remove all the blood, not without also removing much of the color."

That's all it took to stir Faucon's precious bits of information into unfolding. He smiled as he looked upon the whole of the tale they told. It was, indeed, a good day to be alive, especially for Peter the Webber.

When he at last left the stillroom, he gave Colin a message for Brother Edmund, warning his clerk to wait for him here after the mass at Terce ended. In return Colin gave him greetings to share with Stanrudde's shoemakers, should he need something to help him win their compliance.

The abbey's bell began to ring as Faucon exited from the convent's western gate. One by one, the bells of the churches across the city followed suit, their tones ranging from a dark bass to a sweet soprano. The sounds filled the chill air with the reminder to all within Stanrudde's walls that the hour for the Prime mass had come.

He let the carillon carry him in the direction of Father Herebert's church. It was no longer just his need to speak with Peter that drove him, but his own heart's demand for a conversation with his Lord.

All around him, the city stirred mightily, rising swiftly to meet this new day. Roosters crowed, maids sang as they worked, masters shouted at their apprentices. Grunting hogs, chased from their sties, began their daily hunt for offal along the lanes. A great cloud of pigeons rose into the sky, circling and swooping in distress. No doubt the ones who tended these birds had entered their cote to harvest eggs.

Faucon joined the surprisingly large number of folk moving toward Father Herebert's church only to realize that this shorter service would suit city folk, who had so many demands on their day. As he entered the small square where the hue and cry had ended yesterday, he looked to the church porch.

Four men of the town guard stood at either side of the open church door. Rather, they lounged. No doubt having spent the previous night guarding the door, the young men all leaned against the stone wall behind them, their cloaks wrapped tightly around them, eyes closed and faces turned toward the newborn sun.

Ducking his head, Faucon climbed the steps then moved swiftly past them into the church without generating a reaction. That made him wonder if Peter might not be able to do the same going in the opposite direction. As swiftly as he thought it, Faucon set aside the notion. Roger the Webber's son had no desire to become outlaw. Nay, all he wanted was the life that belonged to him, the one that others were just as committed to stealing from him.

Against the possibility that Gisla hadn't yet sent her message to the priest, Faucon eased into the shadows behind the open church door. From that vantage point, he studied the sanctuary. Like most churches as old as this one, it was small, perhaps no more than half as long as Bernart's house, and narrow. Several modest windows pierced the upper reaches of its stone walls. Rather than the arches and rounded ceiling that was the style for churches built more recently, this one's ceiling came to a sharp peak.

Set in a line, three simple columns separated nave from apse, something that would surely change after the new tower was completed. Faucon peered through them, seeking Peter, but couldn't see the webber in his stone seat. Then again, if this church were typical, the frith stool and its sorry occupant would be off to the side of the altar, hidden from Faucon by the angle of the columns.

When the time came for Father Herebert to proceed to the altar, Faucon was startled to see that the sanctuary was nearly full. Folk stood shoulder to shoulder, filling almost the whole space on this side of the columns. As they waited for their priest to begin the service, they chatted with friends, offering those more distant from them waves and calls of *good morrow*.

Yet seeking to remain hidden from the priest, Faucon wound his way into the midst of the crowd, away from the door and the central pathway Father Herebert would use. He pushed past ragged beggars and around well-dressed matrons to stop between a roughhewn workman and an alderman, or so said the gold chain the man wore. It was a good place to stand. There were still enough folk between him and the altar that he would see nothing of the priest at his table, save for the top of Father Herebert's head.

When the elderly churchman raised his rich voice to sing out the opening words of the mass, his rich voice filled the sanctuary, his Latin words both mysterious and familiar in one soaring instant. As always happened, the very cadence of the service lifted Faucon's heart, filling him with comfort and gratitude. His head remained bowed even after it came to an end and he offered up his private thanks for all the wondrous good that presently filled his life.

As the parishioners turned to depart, Faucon let himself be pulled along with them, once again seeking protection behind the door, hoping to prevent or at least delay what might be a confrontation with the priest. Much to his surprise, Father Herebert joined his departing flock, his head bowed. The priest kept his gaze focused at his feet all the way to the door, then stepped through the opening and was gone.

Uncertain if this was Gisla's hand at work or something else, Faucon pushed the door until it was stood barely ajar, then made his way to the apse end of the church. He found Peter the Webber sprawled miserably in the short squat stone chair that was placed between the altar and the wall.

No older than Gisla, Peter looked much like his

father, being long and lanky with blue eyes and fair hair, his skin summer-browned. The lad didn't shift out of his sprawl as Faucon stopped in front of him. Indeed, he seemed barely able to lift his head to see who came. When he finally did, Faucon saw none of his father's anger in his expression. Instead, there was only confusion and fear.

"Peter the Webber, I am Sir Faucon de Ramis, the newly appointed Keeper of the Pleas for this shire. I am the man responsible for resolving the matter of Bernart le Linsman's murder," Faucon told him with a nod of greeting.

Peter's eyes widened. He jerked upright in his stone chair, his hands gripping its hard cold arms. "I have sanctuary," he pronounced without raising his voice.

"Indeed you do," Faucon agreed, "and good it is that you have it. Not because you killed Bernart, for that was not done at your hand. But there remain others outside these walls determined to see you die in their place. They have failed once to achieve their aim, but I have no doubt they'll finish what they began if you do not help me."

The boy stared at him for an instant in astonishment, then released a shaken breath to bury his face in his hands. It was a moment before he again raised his head. To his credit he shed no tears. Instead, there was nothing but gratitude in his gaze.

"Thank you," he breathed. "She saw me trying to help him, even though I knew by looking at his wound it was too late to do aught. I couldn't believe it when she shouted out that I'd done murder. How could anyone believe I'd kill a man I loved like my own father, the man who would one day be my father-by-marriage, especially her?" he pleaded, proving that his father and his friends knew Peter for who he truly was.

"Best you thank God that you had the presence of mind to run rather than staying to argue the point,"

Faucon told him with a laugh.

The boy managed a tiny smile at that, then continued in a stronger voice. "Is she the one who did this horrible thing?"

"I've yet a task or two to do before I can say anything for certain about who made the cut in Bernart's throat as compared to those who planned the cutting. Only after I know all can I free you from this place," Faucon told him. "What I need from you at this moment is your tale. Know before you begin that I've already spoken with Mistress Gisla and she's told me of your private meetings."

This time, Peter's eyes did fill with the moisture from his heart. "Mary save her. She must hate me, believing I used our secret to murder her father."

"You misjudge her," Faucon replied. "I don't think she ever thought, not even for a moment, that you had done this. For your heart's sake you should also know that she had no hand in what happened to her sire. As for your secret, it isn't much of one. So well did those who watched her know what was afoot that they easily discerned which of the two ribbons to place in the stones for you yestermorn."

He smiled down at the young man. "Lastly, you may set aside all thoughts of her hatred, I think. Your little love will happily help your father fulfill the promise he made me at yesterday's inquest. Your sire means to see the two of you wed as soon as possible once your name is cleared."

As Peter heard these words, the boy sagged back into the chair as he shed the greatest of the many worries presently chewing at him. "I pray that day arrives," he muttered, "and when it does, I'll bless it as a miracle.

"As for the tale you want," he continued, "I'm not sure what I have to tell you, save that I came at the hour suggested by our code. If Gisla's held nothing back, then I suppose you know when we met in the workshop I entered by climbing in through that last window."

"So I do," Faucon replied. "But I care less about what happened in the workshop than what occurred as you made your way toward Bernart's home, before you climbed the wall to reach the window. Mistress Gisla told me that you usually came to her on the days when you stopped at Master Hodge's shop."

Peter nodded. "Aye, and that's what happened yesterday. I left fabric for Master Hodge, then made my way toward Master Bernart's house."

"Tell me this. Might Master Hodge have asked you the previous day if you would have fabric for him on the morrow?"

Peter's eyes widened. "He did," he answered in surprise.

"And was the pleykster in his shop when you arrived yesterday?"

"Nay," the boy replied, shaking his head. "I left what I brought with his journeyman. Nory said that his master had departed an hour or more earlier and that he wasn't certain when Master Hodge might return. But as it happened, Master Hodge was on his way back to his shop at that very moment. His path and mine crossed as I wended my way from his shop toward Gisla's home."

"He was carrying something. What was it?" Faucon asked.

Again, the lad eyed him in astonishment. "Aye, he had a sack over his shoulder, but how do you know that?"

Faucon smiled. He knew because the convent's launderers were concerned about removing blood without removing color. "How did he seem to you?"

"Strange," Peter replied. "Not at all like himself. Master Hodge is like my own uncles. There's never been a time when I saw him on a lane that he didn't rush to embrace me, offering greetings and conversation. But yesterday he never looked up as he walked past me, even though I called to him. Perhaps he didn't hear me." Peter's voice trailed off.

Faucon waited for the boy to understand what he already knew, that it had been guilt keeping the master pleykster's gaze fastened to the earth yesterday. It took a moment before Peter blinked.

"You cannot think that Master Hodge had a hand in Master Bernart's death?" Peter protested. "That's not possible. As much as my father now hates Master Bernart with all his heart, Master Hodge loved Gisla's father." Even as Peter tried to convince himself of this, he failed. His brow creased. "But he never looked at me, not even when I called him," he said again.

"What was Master Hodge wearing?" Faucon asked.

That made Peter frown in thought. "His leather apron for sure, but what he had on beneath it I can't say I noticed," he replied uncertainly.

"Ah." Faucon paused as his bits rearranged themselves for a last time. "But he definitely wore his apron?"

Peter nodded. "Of that I'm certain."

"Tell me this," Faucon continued. "Mistress Gisla says that you and she avoided meeting at the hour of None, doing so because she wasn't free, that being the hour of her household's midday meal. She also said that you should have known she wouldn't call you to her at that hour, that you should have known the message false because of that. Why, then, did you come at None?"

The boy shrugged. "I was worried. Gisla and I had talked much about her father's plans, both for her and her mother," he said.

Faucon smiled at that. There was no such thing as a secret in Bernart's house. Save for one.

"Gisla's been so distraught of late that I came even

though I knew the hour was wrong. I feared something awful had finally happened," Peter finished.

"And so it had," Faucon replied. "By any chance did you see someone in the courtyard when you first arrived yesterday?"

Again, astonishment filled Peter's gaze. "How is it you know these things?" he asked. Faucon only shrugged and smiled.

"Aye, I saw Mistress Nanette. She was standing at the corner of the house nearest the kitchen. I ducked beneath the wall as soon as I saw her, but I was certain I moved too late, that she'd already spied me. I crouched there for a moment, even though I expected her to cross the yard and confront me. When that didn't happen, I called myself fortunate and regained my feet to move onto the wall and climb into the window."

He offered Faucon a sour twist of his mouth. "Now you'll tell me that she *had* seen me."

"So I shall," Faucon replied with a laugh, "and so she had. Take heart, Peter the Webber. Although I leave you now, I go promising that I'll be back as soon as I can. As much as I hope that means returning this very day to open the door to your cage, it's possible that may not happen. Should that be the case, take my warning to heart. If you value your life, you'll say nothing of our conversation to anyone, not even to your little love."

Especially not to Gisla. She wouldn't easily bear what she learned out of such sharing. Moreover, she might later unburden her heart to one who didn't deserve her trust.

Peter blanched. "Many thanks," he said weakly. "I am taking your words to heart and will do as you say."

Faucon took a backward step. "One more thing before I leave. Do you by chance know who makes Mistress Gisla's shoes?"

"Why are we here? It's almost noon. I thought you meant us to be on the road to Blacklea after Terce mass was finished," Brother Edmund asked irritably as he shrugged his basket of tools off his shoulder. Setting it on the ground next to the simple wooden table, he sat on the bench across from his employer.

The alewife's house had proved to be of higher quality than Faucon expected, given the clientele mentioned by Temric FitzHenry last night. Standing on the corner where the alley met the chandlers' lane, the woman's two-storey home had bright blue shutters and a sparkling new coat of whitewash. Her yard, a spit of open land between her home and that of her nearest neighbor, was grassy and sprinkled with clumps of late-blooming wildflowers. It was surrounded by hurdles, tall panels made of woven branches and lashed together to form a fence, no doubt serving to protect her neighbors from her customers.

The alewife's son, a disreputable-looking lad with dark hair and eyes, stopped next to Faucon and stretched out his hand. When he received his promised sliver of coin, the boy departed with a wink and a nod.

"That was our agreement last night," Faucon replied, "but dawn shed new light on the matter of Bernart's death. Prepare yourself," he warned his clerk. "This time, we'll be tallying assets and noting values for our king, doing so until your fingers ache all over again."

Faucon couldn't stop his grin as he said these words. By God, this felt right and good. Not only had he run a merry chase to its end, but he would now walk away with the prize he craved.

"What!" Edmund cried out. "You went to the church, leaving me waiting at that lay brother's shed?

How could you take the words of the webber's confession when I wasn't there to record them?! Why didn't you call for me to come with you?" he finished.

The hurt in his clerk's voice made Faucon look askance at the monk. "I didn't call for you because you asked for permission to attend Terce mass and I gave it to you. While you worshiped, I made my way back and forth across this town, seeing this man and that as I found what I needed. I didn't call for you because, on the whole, I didn't know where I was. As for Peter the Webber, aye, I entered the church to speak with him, but not to take his confession. The webber has nothing to confess, save perhaps that he'd been meeting illicitly with Mistress Gisla."

Here, Faucon paused to lift his cup. "Nay, you've missed nothing so far this day, save much walking and a decent cup of ale. Is it a fast day still? If not, would you care for something to eat before we make our way to Bernart's home?"

"I've already broken my fast, sir, doing so with my brothers," Edmund retorted, still aiming his narrow-eyed gaze at his employer. "Something happened. What do you know that I do not?"

That made Faucon laugh aloud. There was so much he knew that Edmund did not. But that wasn't what his clerk meant.

"Nothing worth mentioning has happened since we parted last night, Brother Edmund," he assured the monk, and didn't feel as though he spoke falsely. "When I awoke this morning, I simply saw where this trail leads me. Now here you are at my side as you should be, ready to help me do our duty to king and crown. Know that this is one instance sure to please my uncle."

He offered this last like a honeyed plum, knowing very well how much Edmund wanted to please Bishop William of Hereford. Indeed, the monk's frown instantly disappeared.

"Well then," Edmund said, "we should be off to do as we must." With that, his clerk sprang to his feet as he snatched up his basket's strap. Slinging it over his shoulder, he looked at his employer, blinking rapidly. "My pardon if I seemed to chide a moment ago. That wasn't my intention nor is it my place to do so."

Another apology! And a statement that seemed to indicate Edmund knew his place. Faucon wasn't sure if he should gape or laugh.

"I heard no chiding," he replied as he came to his feet, "only my clerk doing his duty and keeping me within the bounds of the law."

Bending, Faucon reclaimed the hempen sack that lay beneath his bench. As he threw it over his shoulder, he felt very much the city man. "Brother Edmund, if you would please accompany me to Master Bernart's wake. I'll be needing you ready to note any confession that might be made."

Chapter Fourteen

As they'd done yesterday, Faucon and his clerk wended their way through the city to the kinsman's home. With his mind easy, Faucon looked about him, beginning to understand how a man could come to prize such a crowded existence. Overhead the sky was that particular blue given only to autumn, and clear of any sign of rain. The wind was just strong enough to carry away most of the smoke that generally hung like a pall over a place such as Stanrudde.

From every home's lower level window came cries extolling the quality and necessity of the wares made within the shop. Costermongers pushed their carts along the lanes, offering everything from nuts, both shelled and roasted, to soap to salted fat which, the seller proclaimed, would turn even the plainest of potage into a feast. A wee girl sang out a ditty as she offered posies made from autumn flowers and colored leaves. Stubble-fed geese, an autumn delicacy, honked and flapped from where they were tethered to a butcher's window.

At the place where the old city met the new, a dozen men of the town guard waited. Rather than Temric FitzHenry, the man at their head this day was their true captain. A commoner, Otto, son of Otfried, was a gruff old soldier, bald as a babe with but half an ear on the right and a scar that crossed his face from brow to jaw. He hadn't asked Faucon to prove his right to make arrests within this town's walls. Nay, the tale he'd heard of the previous day's inquest had been proof enough for him.

With the guard at his back, Faucon lead the way to where the colorful crowd of folk spilled out through Bernart's gate and into the lane. While the elder folk mingled, chatting as they ate and drank on the richness of the linsman's purse, their youngsters ran along either side the wall, shouting and laughing as they played some game.

"For shame," Edmund muttered as he eyed the happy crowd, "for shame on all of them for laughing and playing. This is no wake. It's a disrespectful show, a perverted fair. Master Bernart died both suddenly and unconfessed. These folk should be on their knees, their hands clasped, as they beg our Lord to help shorten the merchant's stay in Purgatory, especially on this day." It was All Souls Day today.

Faucon glanced at his clerk, a little surprised that the monk wouldn't know that this was the way of wakes held by folk whose souls weren't bound to the Church. "I think Master Bernart didn't much inspire his friends and neighbors to pray on his behalf." Such a courtesy didn't belong to men who broke their word as often as Bernart did.

"Perhaps his term in Purgatory is well earned? As you said yesterday, it's easier to thread a rope through the eye of a needle..." Faucon said, offering half the passage Edmund had quoted.

His clerk looked at him, his brow creased. True concern for the merchant's soul filled his dark eyes. "But they could be helping him. Such frivolity and gluttony on their part is simply wrong."

Faucon couldn't argue that, nor had he any interest in doing so. Instead, he started through the gate, Edmund at his side. As those inside Bernart's courtyard saw their Crowner with the town guard at his back, they fell silent. Even the children ceased their play as they watched their Crowner and his clerk make their way toward the house.

Two of the three tables from the hall now stood near the home's grand doorway. Cheeses, breads and the dishes Mistress Nanette's charges had spent the night creating filled them, along with pitchers of drink. Faucon expected the third table had remained in the hall and that Bernart's linen-wrapped body now lay upon it. If that were so, then the grieving widow had left her daughter and Mistress Nanette to mourn her husband while she attended to her guests.

Alina stood before the half-open door, her stance sideways to him. Once again Faucon noted what he'd almost missed yesterday. Although the widow wore white to pronounce her mourning, there was no sign of yesterday's tears or distress on her face.

Although Mistress Alina hadn't yet noticed him, the man who had no doubt bleached the fabric of her gowns to their present ghostly hue had. Hodge the Pleykster's gaze shifted from his Crowner's face to the sack Faucon carried over his shoulder. He paled, his mouth pinched. His eyes began to water.

Only as Hodge folded his hands as if in prayer did Mistress Alina notice the change in her yard. She shifted, her chin lifting to a haughty angle as she saw her Crowner. There was none of Master Hodge's concern in her gaze. Why, when Alina believed, just as Bernart had, that the silver in her chests gave her power over her own fate?

"Sir Crowner," she called out, "why come you to us this day, bringing these soldiers and disturbing my husband's wake?"

As Faucon halted in front of her, Edmund yet beside him, he lowered his sack to the ground at his feet, making a show of it. "Why, Mistress Alina, I come as is my right and to do my duty to my king. I mean to make my arrest in the matter of your husband's murder."

A surprised murmur rumbled across those

watching, but swiftly died away, leaving only the relentless sound of the city's heartbeat. No one in this yard wanted to miss a word of what came next. Indeed, Faucon wondered if the tale of Bernart le Linsman's wake might live on long after the merchant's legacy was forgotten.

Alina frowned at him. "What do you mean? If you've come here to do that, then I think me you've come to the wrong place. The man who killed my husband is across town, enjoying the benefits of sanctuary, while my husband lies cold and dead in his hall."

"Now mistress," Faucon chided with a shake of his head, "you of all people know that's not true. Peter the Webber couldn't have killed your husband. By the time Roger the Webber's son crawled into the workshop through an open window, Bernart le Linsman was already dead."

This time, there was nothing muted about the sound of surprise that exploded from those watching. Edmund shifted sharply to stare wide-eyed at his employer. Alina paled. Hodge moaned and took a step to the side, as if to distance himself from her, when it was far too late for him to do that.

Behind them, the massive door creaked open. No doubt drawn down the stairs by the change of tenor in the yard, Mistress Gisla stepped outside to join her mother. She also wore white. Today as yesterday, her nose and eyes were reddened in grief for the man Faucon now doubted was her sire.

Mistress Nanette followed Gisla out of the doorway. Unlike mother and daughter, the master needlewoman wore blue. This, when Faucon thought she of all three women ought to be wearing the color of mourning. Save that Nanette had been the one to plan her lover's death.

"Why are you here, Sir Crowner?" Gisla asked, her

voice thick with tears. Then forgetting all caution, she cried, "Has something happened to Peter?"

Faucon offered the girl a quick smile of reassurance, wishing he could spare her these next moments. She didn't deserve what would follow. "Take heart, mistress. Your love is well and safe, and so he will remain. He waits eagerly to fulfill his father's promise as regards your marriage."

Hoping that would be enough for her, Faucon again looked at her mother. "Mistress Alina, who is the father of the child you bear?"

The only sound in the yard was Alina's sharp gasp. She betrayed herself by lowering her hand to cup the slight bulge of her womb.

"You are with child?!" Gisla cried, her face alive with confusion as she stared at her mother.

Hodge swayed, his eyes closed. Only Nanette remained unmoved by this revelation. Instead, she aimed her hard and angry gaze at Faucon.

Alina caught herself and reclaimed her authority. "How dare you speak such words to me on this day of all days? Aye, the Lord granted me a miracle. I am with child. Bernart's child, just Gisla and her brothers were of his line."

Faucon shook his head. "I think not, mistress. I think Bernart's thrusts were empty, that he never had seeds to sow in you, not even when you were first wed. Had he, then I think the woman he preferred would surely have come with child at least once. Yet she never did, not in all the years he used her." As he spoke, he let his gaze shift to Nanette.

Gisla gave a shriek as she understood her Crowner's meaning, and who she was. Lifting her hems, the girl raced away from what remained of her family, rounding the corner of the kitchen to disappear into the garden.

Still Faucon watched Nanette. The master needlewoman stood with her shoulders squared, her spine straight, a soldier preparing for battle when the war was already lost. Her chin lifted until it was at the same angle as the woman who was her better, made so by simple right of birth. Still, she said nothing.

Faucon wondered if Nanette would ever again speak, even on the day the hangman wrapped his noose about her neck. For of the three who had plotted Bernart's death, Nanette alone would be unable to call upon witnesses to speak to her character and prove her innocence. Despite her mastery of her craft, despite the profit she brought into Bernart's home with her needle and through those she trained, she had never been more to him—to anyone who knew her heritage—than the child born to sweep ashes from the hearth. For that reason alone was Bernart now dead.

Hodge was weeping silently now, tears streaming down his face. In the pleykster's reaction Faucon saw there'd be no need to open the sack he carried, the one containing the tunic Hodge had worn when he drew the half-scissor across his dearest friend's throat. Hodge was not as rich as Bernart. Unlike Gisla, he couldn't afford to burn a serviceable garment. Instead, he'd tried to bleach the blood from his tunic. As the launderers at the convent had suggested, all he'd achieved was to remove the color, leaving darkened splotches where Bernart's blood had forever marked his tunic.

Nor did Faucon need to look at Hodge's shoes. It had taken no more than the mere mention of the pleykster's name to Gisla's shoemaker to elicit the man's hearty and disbelieving laugh. Who would ever think that a man as big as Hodge would have so small a foot?

Alina shifted closer to her lover, the father of her children. As she leaned her head upon his shoulder her eyes closed. There was nothing but sadness in her expression. Faucon wondered if she regretted the miracle of her mother and those ribbons given to a queen. If not for them, Hodge might well have been the man her father chose for her. Where Bernart's ambitions would have naturally driven him into a trade that could feed his greed, just as Roger's joy at working with his hands would have sent him seeking out what he now did, there could have been no more straightforward a trade for Hodge than turning linen into braies and head scarves.

Nanette yet stood where she was, silent and still.

Otto, son of Otfriend, joined Faucon. "Is it time, Sir Crowner?"

"It is," Faucon replied, then looked at the three. "Hodge the Pleykster, Alina, daughter of Elinor, Nanette of Stanrudde, I do accuse you of both planning and murdering Bernart le Linsman."

The words struck Hodge like a blow. As he jerked, he set Alina off balance. She stumbled back from him crying out. With a great howling moan, the pleykster pivoted toward Nanette. She sidestepped him, then backed into the doorway and disappeared. Two of the town's soldiers picked up their heels, racing past Faucon to chase her. They need not have hurried. There was no escape for her in Bernart's fine home. Like a dragon's treasure cave, there was only one entrance and exit from the structure.

"This is all on that woman!" Hodge screamed after her. "I wasn't going to do it. I loved him!"

Tears streaming, he looked at Faucon. "But she threatened Alina. She said she'd tell the world the truth about our babes if I didn't ply the blade! I couldn't let her do that."

His fury spent, he collapsed to sit on the courtyard floor. Alina drifted down next to him, taking his hand. He looked at her.

"You know I loved him," he told her. "I loved him as much as I love you. I swear I wasn't going to do it. I wouldn't have done it if she hadn't put the damned scissors in my hands."

With that, the last unsettled piece in Faucon's mind slipped into its proper place. He would find Rob's missing bolt in Nanette's possession. When Alina had returned from the workshop that second time, doing so in distress, Nanette had left the table to do what her mistress could not and force Hodge to do the deed as he promised. It was Nanette who had taken the scissors from Rob's table and parted them outside the workshop. It was she who had put the separated tool into Hodge's hands before sending him into Bernart's workroom to kill her lover.

Chapter Fifteen

"**I** still don't understand how you knew that all three together had arranged the linsman's death, Sir Faucon," said Abbot Athelard. The Churchman was middle-aged, portly and good-natured, his hair so thin and fair that it was hard to tell where his tonsure ended and his hair began. He wore a simple habit, albeit decorated around the sleeves with needlework that wasn't as fine as that done at Bernart's house.

As the abbot spoke, he picked up his bejeweled cup and sipped at his wine. A wave of his hand indicated that Faucon should do the same. "Do you understand it, Oswald?" Athelard asked of the other man with whom Faucon had shared this rich meal.

Oswald de Vere, Bishop William of Hereford's grandnephew and private secretary, was the august visitor for whom the abbot had held aside the guest house. Although ten years Faucon's senior, there was no mistaking that he and Oswald were kin. Nay, they were more than kin, they were de Veres. They shared the same black hair and dark eyes, lean cheeks and long nose, both of them hiding the too-pointed chin given to the family under a neatly-trimmed beard.

Faucon's cousin stared distractedly down into the remains of his meal. Although trained in the Church, Oswald was no monk. Indeed, as Faucon watched his cousin, he was grateful that his mantle and pin were of good enough quality to make him seem less of a ragtag relation. Oswald wore his own clothing, a fine red tunic beneath a rich blue mantle. The purple stones in the pin that held his outer garment in place sparked in the light of the dozen candles the abbot used to restrain the shadows in his private hall.

"Oswald?" Faucon prodded when his cousin still didn't offer an answer to the abbot's question.

The older man looked up with a start. "What did you say, Pery?" he asked, using Faucon's pet name, Pery being short for Peregrine, a play on the meaning of Faucon.

"The abbot was asking about the three who plotted to murder the linsman," Faucon said. It wasn't like Oswald to drift, especially when there was an influential man at the table with him.

"My pardon. My thoughts wandered for a moment. So tell us. How did you know?" Oswald asked, bringing his attention back to the abbot and his future.

"It was how Mistress Alina told the tale of finding her dead husband in the workshop. She and Mistress Nanette were very careful about the story, relying on each other to supply pieces. Later, when I heard Mistress Gisla tell her side of the tale, I found they'd done the same to her, making sure she knew only what they wanted her to know.

"And then there was the matter of the tally sticks," Faucon added with a laugh. "Neither of the women spoke a word when I asked why Master Bernart's tally sticks might have been locked away if the linsman was hard at his counting. They couldn't say anything. Mistress Alina didn't know Nanette had locked away the sticks after the pleykster had done the deed. Since Mistress Alina couldn't say anything about it, neither could Mistress Nanette, not without potentially contradicting the other or revealing something untoward."

He grinned at Oswald. "When you next see our uncle, tell him that this was an incredibly successful day for him. Mistress Alina's estate is all I anticipated, while even the pleykster's meager trade proved to have more value than I would have imagined."

The man who'd seen to it that Faucon received that parchment and wax seal testifying to Faucon's rights as Coronarius offered a weak grin at that. "I knew you would do well at this, Pery. I said as much to our uncle when he told me he'd settled on you as the first of the Coronarii for this shire. Well done."

At the head of the table, the abbot nodded, offering another warm smile. "Although I wasn't initially convinced our shire needed such a man, not when we already have a sheriff, I must admit you're changing my mind, Sir Faucon. I doubt Sir Alain could have done as well with the linsman's murder, or have brought the matter to a close so swiftly. Only two days, Sir Faucon, and peace is restored to our city. Well done, indeed."

"You are kind to say so, Father Abbot," Faucon said, very much enjoying what he'd just stolen from Sir Alain. Aye, if he'd been the hare in this encounter, then, as hares were occasionally wont to do, he'd just delivered a vicious and stunning blow to the fox who chased him.

Colin's plum wine was tasty and heady. Faucon lifted his horn cup in salute to the brewer, then took a second sip. The monk grinned, and raised his own simple wooden bowl to his lips and drank.

A half dozen tallow lamps again sat upon Colin's cluttered table, their flames jigging and dancing as they drove back the depths of night. The monk had just returned from singing the Compline service. After redressing Faucon's back, he'd offered this potent stuff as a way of celebrating his Crowner's success this day. What else was there to do at this hour save enjoy each other's company until Colin left to celebrate Matins and

Faucon at last sought out his pallet?

"I'm glad she's gone to stay at Roger the Webber's home, rather than returning to her own bed," Faucon said of Gisla. "That house will be a painful place for her from now on, I think."

Alina's daughter had run to Peter when she left the wake, where she'd wept out the whole tale to her love. To Roger's credit he'd already stated that it made no difference to him if the girl who wed his son were Bernart's child or Hodge's bastard. Not that Faucon didn't think it was greed driving the webber. After all, Gisla was still heir to all her mother owned, and that was everything, since none of it had ever been Bernart's to pass along. Moreover, the skills Gisla had learned at Bernart's knee could only improve any man's estate.

"So what do you think? Will she part with coin to see her mother released?" Colin asked. "I say she will."

The guard had taken Bernart's murderers to the town's sole keep tower, the place that served as Stanrudde's gaol. There the three would stay until someone paid the fees required to restore their freedom.

"Her mother for certain," Faucon agreed. "But not Mistress Nanette, I think. I cannot know this, but I suspect it was at Nanette's insistence that Alina lied about the plans for Gisla to marry Peter. With Peter dead, the two planned to see Gisla wed to that London goldsmith. With Alina's heir removed, Nanette could have then moved the trade to some other place, perhaps even London, making an alliance of her own with that mercer. That would have left Alina free to marry Hodge."

Faucon shook his head as he thought of the pleykster. "I expect he'll have to fund his own release as well, having no kith or kin of his own."

"And you're certain that the coins were left on the board as a payment for Sir Alain?" Colin asked, once more shaking his head, this time at how blatantly their sheriff's aid could be purchased.

"Aye, I'm certain. That's why the tally sticks were locked away," Faucon said, emptying his cup. "Nanette didn't want to give Sir Alain any chance to discover just how rich Bernart was. Like many men, I expect Bernart was paying less than he owed his king in tax, thus also shorting Sir Alain." Alain's pay was a percentage of the tax he collected.

Nor did Faucon doubt that Alina's message to Sir Alain about her husband's death had gone out the day before Bernart had died. He wondered how she'd conveyed to Alain what she'd wanted from him, if she'd stated it boldly or if there were some sort of ribbon that told a corrupt sheriff the coins on the bloody board were his once he'd rendered the correct verdict.

However, unlike those who plotted Bernart's death, Alain knew he'd never even see those coins. That hadn't stopped him from using Alina's warning to set his dogs on his new Crowner. Colin poured a little more wine in his own cup, then offered more to his Crowner. Faucon shook his head, although in regret. The morrow would come too soon. It wouldn't do to ride four hours to Blacklea on the morrow with an aching head, not when those same dogs might be waiting for him along the way.

"I take it your pattern found its mate this morning," Colin said as he rose to put the jug back on one of his many shelves.

Faucon laughed at that. "Do you know, I never took those linen bits from my purse? I asked Peter who made Gisla's shoes, just because I had to start somewhere. By the bye, William the Shoemaker returns your greetings with his own, thanking you again for that concoction you last gave him."

"Do you mean to say you never even asked after Alina's pattern from Will?" Colin asked in surprise.

Faucon gave a quick lift of his brows at that, his smile pleased. "I wasn't looking for Alina's pattern, or Nanette's even though she's the taller woman. Nay, I simply walked into the man's shop, offered your greeting and asked about Hodge the Pleykster. That's when your shoemaker started laughing, and told me the tale of a big man with small feet."

The monk's brow creased at that. "But how did you know?" he demanded. "I was so certain it was Alina who did this. Moreover, what of it if Hodge's feet are small for his size? How could you know he was the one you sought, if you didn't match your pattern to the one Will has in store?"

"Because Bernart's workshop table was so tall and, consequently, so was his stool," Faucon replied. This had been one of the insights that had awakened him this morn. "All day yesterday the idea of a smaller man slashing Bernart's throat bothered me, although I couldn't say why. Then last night, your Richard Alwynason ended the life of one of my attackers with the same stroke. It wasn't until I'd slept on both deaths that I understood what I'd missed in the workroom. Bernart's stool had him sitting high and the cut across throat started high. That meant the man behind him had to have been tall enough to start the cut from that point. Neither woman could have dealt that blow from such a starting position."

Faucon turned his cup in his hand, staring into its empty depths as he shook his head. "Even more importantly, I don't think Master Bernart would have allowed either his wife or his leman to come up behind him, not without turning to look at her. He was angry with Alina because he couldn't be shed of her and angry with Nanette, who had unreasonably expected them to continue running their trade together once he took it to London. She may even have expected him to marry her, something I'm sure he would have cruelly refused to do.

In his mind, she was barren and he wanted a son. And perhaps a younger wife."

Then Faucon raised his empty cup to once more salute the monk. "Nay, I cornered my prey because of you, who knows this town like his own face. You told me there was only one man left in Stanrudde whom Bernart hadn't betrayed. Thus, Master Hodge was the only one Bernart would trust enough that he wouldn't look up when that man came to stand behind him. What makes this ironic is that Hodge was, in fact, the one man who had betrayed Bernart, doing so over and over as he bedded Alina. He'd even set his own seed into her womb because Bernart could not."

The praise had Colin grinning. He made a show of tugging at a forelock he didn't own. "My thanks, Sir Crowner. Glad I am that I could be of assistance." Then he sobered. "Will any of them hang for what they did, do you think?"

"Who's to say?" Faucon replied with a sigh, almost regretting that delivering the punishment owed to murderers wasn't one of his duties as a servant of the crown. Nay, his only purpose was to identify them and confiscate the king's portion of what they owned.

"Were I to guess, I'd say Nanette will," he continued. "Unlike Peter, whose witnesses came forward immediately to pronounce his innocence, there'll be no one she can call to swear to her character. Even if she protests that she wasn't Bernart's leman, using the fact that she's never come to childbed, she remains an unwed woman. Now that the charge of fornication has been made, she'll be stained forever by it, no matter the truth." For that reason, Faucon was glad of his certainty before he'd labeled her thusly.

"Hodge will call his witnesses and they will come," Colin said. "He has many friends in this town."

Faucon nodded. So he'd seen at the hue and cry. "He could, but I think he won't. His guilt is destroying him," he countered. "Moreover, Hodge has already admitted he did the deed, speaking the words for everyone at Bernart's wake to witness. He even went so far as to state that Nanette forced his hand by threatening Alina. Nay, if anyone lives beyond this act, it will be Alina. That she'll do only because I know how much silver she has in store."

"Poor Alina," Colin murmured. "Unlike her daughter, she will never marry the one to whom she gave her heart." He shook his head as if he grieved for Bernart's widow when Faucon wasn't certain the woman deserved it.

"Save for Gisla and Peter, who aren't yet wed, I don't know anyone who ever has married to please their hearts," Faucon replied, shooting a quizzical look at the old man.

"I did," the monk replied and smiled.

epilogue

Although Faucon had intended to get an early start for Blacklea the next morning, Abbot Athelard had insisted he remain to share the midday meal. With no answer acceptable to the churchman save 'aye,' Faucon lingered until it was well after Sext when he finally convinced Athelard that it wasn't safe for any man to ride home in the dark.

After sending a message to Edmund that they'd be on the road in a half an hour, he went to the stable to see to his courser. Legate had enjoyed two days filled with hay and oatcakes, and even raised a complaint when his master began to check his shoes. But by the time Faucon had his saddle in place, his big white steed had resigned himself to returning to their more rural life.

"Sir Crowner? Oh, please be here," a man called.

Faucon turned, his hands still working the saddle's girth. "I am here," he called back, lifting his head to see who came.

It was a young man dressed in blue and red. Faucon frowned a little, recognizing that color combination from the inquest, but not the household that used it.

The journeyman stopped beside him. "Sir Crowner, I come to you from Richard, son of Alwyna. He bids me tell you that, much to his surprise, he finds himself in need of your assistance. He reminds you of the bargain you two made." The young man paused, his face filling with confusion. "He says I should tell you that two dead men travel to the abbey and Master Richard is need of a cesspit."

Faucon stared at the man, beyond surprise. Two days? This, when Temric had seemed so certain he'd never see his repayment.

At his reaction, the journeyman shook his head and lifted his hands. "I know, his words seemed mad to me as well. But I vow to you, that's exactly what he said to me. He said I was to say his words back to you in the same way. You should know that he's injured with a broken rib," the young man added, "so perhaps his mind is affected by pain."

That stirred a quiet laugh from Faucon. "Dead men making their way to the abbey? Now that's something I need to see. Do they walk or ride? On which road do these corpses make their gruesome journey?"

"Master Richard didn't say," the soon-to-be tradesman offered, sounding flustered. "But the master and his wife were traveling to Bristol when they found these dead men."

Faucon blinked. Temric FitzHenry wasn't married, or at least he hadn't been when last Faucon visited Graistan. And if Faucon's guess was right, chances were those traveling corpses had been breathing men when Temric first encountered them. This story got more interesting by the moment.

"Then I expect the Bristol road is where I'll find these wandering corpses," Faucon said with a nod, then laughed again. "Dead men traveling. Tell your Master Richard he can rest easily. I'll find him his cesspit."

all Souls day

I have broken all the bonds that should hold me. On this day, when I should be with my own family, chanting prayers for the dead, begging our Lord to lift the countless hapless souls trapped in Purgatory into Paradise, I am here, watching her. But is she not also lost here, trapped in this earthly Purgatory? Do I not have the ability to give her heavenly Paradise? These are the lies I tell myself. My Master bade me stay my hand, but, sinner that I am, I cannot bear to do so, not when I know the corruption that awaits her. I have the power to save her.

Hidden in the barren branches of a coppiced tree, I watch her race around her family's fine home. Even in play, our Father's light streams from her, once again calling to me. Her features are fine far beyond the crudeness of her life. Her skin is flawless, her hair a glorious golden-red.

I cannot fail her. She will have her heavenly reward.

a note from Denise

Thank you for reading this second book of my new mystery series. I hope you enjoyed Faucon and his second investigation as his shire's new Crowner. If you liked the book, or I suppose even if you didn't, consider leaving a review. If you've found any formatting or typographical errors, please let me know by email at denisedoming@gmail.com. I appreciate the chance to correct my mistakes!

I have to admit I once again totally enjoyed following Faucon, Colin and Edmund on their most recent next investigation. For anyone wondering, the idea of Alina and her 'woman's' trade, I read about the women's guilds of Paris, which included embroidery as a trade. After looking at so many manuscript illustrations and Medieval paintings showing intricate designs on tunics and gowns, it occurred to me that Paris and nunneries weren't the only place where women were making their living with a needle. Thus the purchase of embroidery ribbons by the dowager Queen Eleanor created by her namesake, Mistress Elinor.

I couldn't resist adding just a peek into Sir Alain's mind in this book. Truth be told, when I first conceived of this series, Alain's voice was the one in my head. Then Faucon came along and everything changed.

By the way, you'll find Temric of Graistan, Oswald de Vere, Brother Colin and Bishop William in my Seasons series.

glossary

This book includes of number of Medieval terms. I've defined the ones I think might be unfamiliar to you. If you find others you'd like defined, let me know at denisedoming@gmail.com and I'll add them to the list.

Braies   A man's undergarment. Made from a single piece of linen that is tied around the waist with a cord. Worn more or less like a loin cloth but more voluminous so the garment can be arranged to cover the hips and thighs.

Chausses   Stockings made of cloth (not knitted). Each leg ties onto the waist cord of the braies.

Crowner   From the Latin *Coronarius*, meaning Servant of the Crown. The word eventually evolves into 'Coroner'

Dower   The bridegroom's offering to his bride. Generally dower should be one-third the value of the bride's dowry. Dower is an annuity for the wife, meant to support her after her husband's death. She holds her dower for her life time, and can accrue dower over the course of multiple marriages. Upon her death, her dower returns to the heirs of the original owner.

Dowry   What the bride brings to her husband upon marriage. Depending on her class, this can be a throne, estates, a skill (such as needlework), or in the case of peasant brides, pots and pans and other household goods.

Hauberk   A heavy leather or padded vest, sometimes sewn with steel rings. Usually worn in place of a chain mail tunic by common soldiers

Hemp   A soft, strong fiber plant with edible seeds. Hemp can be twisted into rope or woven for use in making everything from storage bags to mattress covers.

Pleas of the Crown
    The list of pleas made for justice from the king or his representative from the royal court. No unlike the list of crimes and complaints filed at your local police station.

Toft and Croft A toft is the area of land on which a peasant's house sits. The croft, generally measuring seven hundred feet in length and forty in width. It was in the croft that a serf would grow their personal food staples, such as onions, garlic, turnips and other root crops, legumes and some grains.

Withe   A thin, supple willow (but also hazel or
               ash) branch

25433759R00109

Made in the USA
San Bernardino, CA
30 October 2015